American Law

A Law Novel

Camille Taylor

American Law

Limitless Publishing, LLC
Kailua, HI 96734
www.limitlesspublishing.com

Formatting: Limitless Publishing

ISBN-13: 978-1-68058-449-3
ISBN-10: 1-68058-449-9

Dedication

For my wonderful grandparents.

Prologue

May 2011
The Pentagon, Virginia, USA

Secretary of Defense Walter Mann sat at his desk in his private office at the Pentagon, long after midnight. The other employees had long since gone home. He was completely alone, the cleaners having come and gone hours ago. The security guards never patrolled this area of the building, since the information kept here was highly classified. Silence surrounded him except for the gentle hum of his computer and the tapping of the keys as he typed.

He removed his Ralph Lauren glasses and blinked, his tired eyes stinging. He pinched the bridge of his nose. He'd been in the military for the past forty years and had earned his high position within the government through hard work and dedication. He had started at the bottom and proved himself every step of the way.

He had made his way up the ladder fast, leap

frogging over other candidates, determined to make something out of his life. He had taken all the difficult jobs that would set him out in a crowd, preparing himself for greatness from the start. Now, he was *the* man at the Pentagon who directly reported to the White House.

He had denied himself a lot of opportunities in life to get where he was. He had never married, never had children. Some might have considered his life bleak, empty, but he considered it to be quite full and important. A lot of people knew who he was and revered him. Young, green soldiers looked to him as a role model, a man they would want to be when they reached his age. He had given his country all he had; it meant everything to him and he would protect it at all costs.

He had joined the military at the first possible instance once he became of legal age and never had any doubts, not once looking back or regretting any decision, never wishing things had gone differently.

He stared at his flat computer screen as he imputed the details of the file. The bright light irritated his eyes but he had to get the job over and done with. He ignored the harsh glare and swallowed the last of his coffee that had since gone cold. He had never been a tech person, but he had learned all about computers and technology purposely so he could understand his juniors when they spoke. He refused to let anyone talk down to him.

He liked to know what and how things were going on in his house, and the Pentagon was *his* house. There was no mistake about that. Nothing went on that he didn't know about. He had even gone as far as installing an invisible key stoke logger that recorded everyone's daily activities. He didn't see it as spying, more like a worried father checking up on a wayward teenage daughter, keeping her safe within his home.

He knew others would not see it that way and would cry about their civil rights or some such bullshit, and they would be right. Which was why he was the only one who knew about it. There were a lot of things that the employees of DoD didn't know about and that was the way he liked it—much like the public didn't know half of the things their government had gotten involved in. Ignorance was bliss, as they say.

It had been quite some time since he had done this type of data entry and would usually leave it for his assistant to do but the file's contents were sensitive. No one else was allowed to see what went into the folder marked **'*Sundown.*'** It was for his eyes only. Well, his and the President of the United States, along with the National Security Advisor, and a few others high up within the White House, those who often sat in on the discussions in the Oval Office.

Sundown had taken months to research and implement and was currently the foremost security protocol for the United States. The ideas had already become law and regulation in most of the country's fifty states.

He continued to enter the information. This was no trial run; the future of the country sat before him, and must be kept away from prying eyes and those who would use the contents of the file against them. The information included contingency plans for events such as acts of terrorism and Armageddon.

He finalized the file, entering the data in numerical format, then closed it, adding the security protection to the folder and saving it to the Pentagon's central mainframe. He buried it deep beneath the budgets and fire evacuation forms where it would be safe. His job was to protect the information in the file with his life. There was no other option. If someone stole the contents of Sundown and sold it, or used the data for their own means, the effects could be catastrophic. The country would be defenseless against attack.

He shook his head, unable to agree with the decision makers on that subject. He didn't like that their country's safety sat in one plan—in one file. He certainly didn't like the fact that everything had been carefully detailed in the file. But he had been overruled.

He only prayed that Sundown would remain hidden, buried deep down inside the mainframe where no one would ever find it.

Chapter 1

Three Months Later…
Somewhere over the Atlantic

The Rossiya Airline Boeing 767 plane travelled through turbulence, and Dmitry Ivanov gripped the armrest of his chair, hard, trying to relax. He inhaled deeply then exhaled slowly, thinking of anything but the fact that he was thirty-five thousand feet in the air, relying on the engineering of the plane to hold, the engine to remain in working order, and a well-trained pilot at the controls. His brain worked hard to handle the stress, taking in the specs of the plane and brought them together revealing how a plane was able to soar across the open sky.

He began comparing or breaking down information logically, trying to find solace. Dmitry hated flying and he especially hated turbulence. He could feel the contents of his stomach churn as sweat beaded on his forehead. He dabbed at his face with the napkin leftover from dinner. His friend,

Ivan Anisimov, chuckled from where he sat beside him in the cramped economy section.

Dmitry glared at him, not daring to move much in case it caused the tasteless airplane food to return.

"Can it, man," he snapped.

Ivan grinned, the bastard enjoying his suffering. He'd never been much of a flyer and Ivan was always happy to point it out. He'd known Ivan since they were small boys. Up until the age of sixteen, when they discovered girls, they had been inseparable. Ivan's goal had always been to make a quick buck, having tried every scheme possible. Unfortunately, he never had much luck or enough money, at least until recently when he and Dmitry had started a business together. Using Dmitry's computer expertise and Ivan's fast talking, they were doing really well and it was completely legal—a new detail for Ivan.

While their business had been mostly contained in Russia, with a few odd jobs in the Ukraine and Estonia, this was the first time in which they had been requested to cross the Atlantic Ocean. While the job sounded interesting, and he could play tourist once it was completed, Dmitry began second guessing the decision.

He placed his palm on his stomach and prayed he would not embarrass himself by throwing up. They were six hours into the flight, after catching a connecting flight in Paris before continuing toward Washington D.C. Another five hours would pass before they touched down at Dulles International Airport. He hoped he wouldn't have any lasting ill effects, since they had a meeting at eight the next morning.

It would be their first international job. He and Ivan were still in the process of building up their business, and reputation meant everything to the type of people Dmitry wanted to attract. Tomorrow had to run smoothly. He still had no idea how Ivan had managed to sweet-talk the clients into bringing them over from Russia—all expenses paid—when a local company could have done the same work they were asking for. He wasn't about to argue. The client planned to expand their small business, and if they played their cards right, hopefully they would give them a glowing recommendation, allowing them to go farther in their own industry.

Dmitry closed his eyes and tried to sleep. He didn't usually like to waste valuable time; he could be working on one of his many trademark firewalls or security programs. But the motion of the airplane wasn't conducive to concentrating, and his laptop screen would more than likely make him even sicker.

Some four hours later, he remained wide awake. He had begun reviewing code in his head after he found that sleep was evading him. Making internal notes of what he would need to fix or update when he got a chance. Ones and zeros rotated about in his mind.

He never knew where the talent for computers had come from. His sister, Elena, certainly wasn't technology-minded. He had just been born with the gift and used it to his advantage, the elite programming appearing in his head while he slept.

The fasten seat-belt sign came on and he felt the landing gears beneath them extend. He let out a calming breath as the pilot began the descent. Thank God for that. Any longer and they would have had a crazy person on board. Beside him, Ivan sat up in his seat and wiped the drool from his mouth. The man could sleep anywhere.

"We there yet?" Ivan asked, sounding groggy. He yawned, his jaw cracking.

Dmitry shook his head. "Almost."

"Get any sleep?" Ivan glanced at him with a critical eye.

Dmitry wondered fleetingly what he looked like; it couldn't have been pretty after the eighteen hours of airsickness he had just suffered through. "No, not yet. I'm too wired. That, and the airsickness didn't exactly let me rest."

Ivan nodded, clearly understanding through the haze of sleep. He was beginning to wake up. "Well, we'll be at the hotel soon and you can rest there."

The thud of the tires against the tarmac had his muscles relaxing. About time. He was about to go stir crazy. He might be a bit claustrophobic. It would certainly explain some things. As soon as the seat-belt sign turned off, Dmitry shot out of his seat. He collected his carry-on and was halfway down the aisle before Ivan had even stood.

Another forty-five minutes, and he got through customs and immigration. Another twenty and he and Ivan were driving out of Budget Car Rentals in a black Ford Focus. Ivan took the wheel and turned on the GPS. Ivan never asked for directions, but had always been comfortable letting a computer tell him where to go. Dmitry refrained from commenting as he listened to the computerized voice telling Ivan to continue east on I-66 toward the center of D.C., and eventually to the Marriot Hotel near Dupont Circle where he and Ivan would be staying. Their route bypassed the White House, and if it hadn't been so late in the evening he would have asked Ivan to make a detour and drive down Pennsylvania Avenue so he could have a look. But instead, they continued on, weaving through the late night traffic.

Outside, the scenery blurred as they sped by, the landscape so different from home it was almost alien. Dmitry had lived in Moscow his entire life. He and Elena's parents were working class who had done everything they could to further their children's lives and education. Unfortunately for them, they had passed away before either of them could see the successes their children became.

Ivan slowed the car as they neared a fender bender, merging into the lane beside them when it was clear that the motorists required no help from them. Dmitry leaned back in his seat. He had known he would be coming here, but the reality of it had only begun to sink in. He'd always thought he would visit Elena in D.C., but she hadn't moved there like he'd anticipated. He took a deep breath, letting the polluted smog-filled air into his lungs, and for the first time was happy about it. He'd had enough of breathing in the regulated stale airplane oxygen.

He thought about what he needed to do and wondered if he would get a chance to take a look around Washington before he flew back home.

Maybe he could tell Elena what she'd been missing. He already had a list of things he wanted to see, such as the Ford Theatre and Lincoln Memorial. The Washington Monument was also featured. He only hoped that this job wouldn't take up the entire week.

The Marriot was a large brownstone. An attendant stood at the check-in desk, despite their late arrival. The young man appeared bright and chipper—probably due to the coffee cup sitting on the desk. He quickly found their reservation, and handed them a couple of electronic swipe keys. The two double beds in their shared room, however uninviting with their floral designs, were the best things he had seen in a long time.

He made his way to the bed furthest from the door and dropped his luggage down between the bed and wall. He opened the nearby window, letting in the city air as he looked out at Washington's nightlife. The pretty lights failed to excite him. He was utterly exhausted from the flight. On the other hand, Ivan appeared well-rested, his eyes alight with mischief.

"So are you up for hitting the streets of D.C.?" he asked. "Doing some partying, hopefully also some American woman?"

He shook his head. "*Nyet*, I want to be fresh for the morning. You go ahead. I'm just going to call Elena before I crash."

His sister worried a lot about him these days, having lost her husband to a traitor and then a potential lover to his home country. She feared losing him, too. Since their parents had died, he and

Elena were the only family either of them had left.

Ivan shrugged. "Okay, but you don't know what you're missing."

He knew exactly what he was missing, and was quite happy to stay at the hotel. He and Ivan's tastes were entirely different and he, for one, had never woken up in a foreign jail cell sleeping off the night before, with no recollection as to what he'd done that caused him to be arrested.

"I'm sure I can guess," he said, yawning. "And if not, you'll certainly tell me. See you in the morning."

Ivan gave him an exaggerated wink. "All right. I'll try to keep it down when I get back."

He turned toward the adjoined bathroom to prepare himself for lady catching. He had an entire routine he completed before heading out on the town, all in an attempt to maximize his return. Ivan left broken hearts in his wake, or at least a trail of one-night stands and names and faces he would never remember. Ivan's last long-term relationship lasted about two weeks.

Dmitry flopped down on his bed and stretched out. He lifted the hotel's handset and dialed the international number. Moscow was eight hours ahead of D.C., so he hoped to catch Elena before she left for work as a liaison officer for SVR, Russia's version of the CIA. She had worked at the Yasenevo office for over five years now, and had married her then supervisor Nikolai Nagregor shortly after joining the agency. Their bliss had been short lived; two years ago, Nikolai had been murdered by a close friend and fellow agent.

Dmitry hoped his sister would have another chance of happiness with CIA agent Lucas Gates, who had followed a terrorist to Russia where he met Elena. But eighteen months later, she remained in Moscow and Lucas stayed in America. Dmitry had often tried talking to Elena about him, but she always shut him down and changed the subject. His sister, the Queen of Denial.

The phone rang in his ear and kicked over to Elena's voicemail. He must have just missed her.

Dmitry cleared his throat before speaking after the beep. "Hi, Elena, sorry I missed you. Just letting you know I arrived safely. I'm at the Marriot now, about to hit the sack. Talk to you later."

He hung up the phone, deciding to try her again later if he found the time and if he remembered. The important thing was that she knew he'd gotten there safely. He had already organized a wake-up call with the front desk, not wanting to rely on his cell to wake him. He knew he would more than likely hit the snooze button if it was left up to him. They couldn't be late for their meeting; it was too important.

He yanked off his shoes and crawled beneath the covers, not bothering to brush his teeth before bed. It was past midnight and he could feel his eyelids getting heavy. He was asleep within minutes and didn't even stir when Ivan exited the bathroom and left the room.

Chapter 2

Elena Ivanova climbed out of her shower and brushed her teeth. She dressed in a pressed charcoal grey dress with a navy blue suit jacket over the top as she slipped into her polished black flat boots. She pulled her light brown, or sometimes dark blonde hair—depending on the light—into a chignon, adding clips to keep it in place. Making her way into the kitchen, she poured coffee from the carafe into her SVR stamped mug, and surveyed her apartment.

Nothing had changed in years. She hadn't bought new furniture or even new cushions. The bed she slept in was the same one she had shared with her husband. She and Nikolai had made the apartment a home, and the now dreary place had been filled with life. It remained her first real home, the home she was supposed to live in for the rest of her life. The home she had planned to raise children in, with Nikolai. That would never happen now.

Elena remembered running about the stores in Moscow looking for the perfect draperies. As a newlywed, she'd been disappointed in her husband's lack of interest in the job so she had decorated in colors she knew would give him a heart attack. She wasn't an overly feminine woman, yet the place looked like a Barbie dream house. It certainly screamed female; even a gay man wouldn't have been caught dead in their apartment.

She had expected Nikolai to say something, but he had been happy with it—at least as far as she could tell. He hadn't cared, so long as she didn't touch his office. His response had certainly given her pause and she soon learned that not much rattled her new husband. Eventually they had grown to live with the soft baby pink and white lace décor, and now, years after his death, she had been seriously considering selling and getting another place. The apartment was too full of memories, both good and bad, and she thought it time to move on.

She noticed the blinking red light on her answering machine, indicating that she had a message, and immediately crossed the room to press the play button. Her insides clenched, her heart speeding up involuntary as she held her breath. Dmitry's voice sounded out, and her heart sunk. She had been hoping, praying for another's voice.

She hadn't heard from Lucas in over a month and had started to worry. She wondered if he had changed his mind, deciding that he no longer wanted to wait for her. She didn't even want to think of the other reason—that he had found someone else. She knew Lucas wouldn't wait forever, but she still had trouble taking the plunge. Giving everything she was to him would take

14

time...time she probably didn't have if the scenarios playing in her head were true. She tried to shake off her doubts, but little insecurities had etched themselves into her subconscious.

She had been extremely lonely in the past few months. Dmitry spent all his time with his childhood friend Ivan. Her own friends had long since left her, having cut them off after Nikolai died. She'd not wanted company of any kind and had spent a long time trying to come to grips with her grief. The rest had left after she had thrown them to the curb. She didn't know who she could trust anymore, the hurt of betrayal clouding her senses. She considered seeing a psychiatrist, hoping to clear up the matter. Not that the last one had helped any. She had been ordered to see one after Nikolai had been murdered, and had originally been opposed to the idea. She had become a hermit, and her life consisted only of going to work and then coming home.

She knew she had to get out of her rut, but the few people she could trust were all currently in America. Carey Madigan-Thomas had moved back home a couple of years ago, shortly before Nikolai had died. She and Elena had met after Carey had gone to SVR, determining that most of the artifacts in the Kremlin Armory had been fakes. The Russian mob had substituted the real ones and sold them on the black market.

Carey had lost her husband, Alan, not long after, and Elena had felt for her, working hard to get the perpetrator convicted. It hadn't worked well. The Brotherhood took care of their own or sent them out for a cement swim, whichever the case. No charges were brought and Elena had felt like she had betrayed Carey in some way. Alan Thomas deserved justice, and she'd been unable to get that for him.

Lucas had followed Carey not long after the joint CIA-SVR case they'd worked on had closed. He returned with his arm in a sling, back to the CIA where they had swapped the occasional email or telephone call—or at least they had until a month ago. She had used her contacts in the United States to find out if Lucas was all right when she hadn't heard from him, and after learning he was fine had begun to panic. Her thoughts were a riot as she tried to wrap her head around the reasons he had not contacted her.

Now her own brother was there and she couldn't help but feel as if they were all abandoning her, leaving her alone in Russia. She knew she was being silly; her friends and family had lives of their own to live, and in a way, she felt happy for each of them in their own ventures. She was the only one holding herself back. She stayed behind while the others moved forward.

Dmitry had once said she kept her head in the sand. That she was too afraid to live her life, to move on from Nikolai and give her relationship with Lucas a shot. He was right. She felt scared; she didn't deny that, but acceptance was only the first step. She still had plenty more to go before she could do anything about it. She was a work in progress. Elena took a deep breath and focused on the deep voice booming out of her answering machine.

She smiled as Dmitry told her he had arrived safely. Her brother had known she would fret until she got word from him. Now she could go to work and concentrate on her cases without having to worry about him. He was a good brother, kind and considerate. She hoped he had a great time while he was there. Elena only prayed Ivan would not lead her brother astray and get him into trouble.

Chapter 3

Sean Henry looked about the richly decorated office from his seat in the plush visitor's chair, at the deep cobalt blue carpet beneath his feet and the stormy grey walls, with expensive prints framed of the city adding a splash of color. He would never be able to work in a place like this, but at least he was better off now than he had been. He waited patiently for the boss to finish his phone call, while admiring the artwork and wondering if he could manage to escape with a few of them under his arm. They would fetch a good price.

He knew all the right people; he could make an under-the-counter sale and walk away with a hefty wad of cash. However, he couldn't entertain such thoughts. There would be a time, hopefully in the near future, that he would no longer need the old man. Until then, it was best not to bite the hand that fed him.

His fake ID got him into the building, since his real one would have shown his multiple arrests from the time he was eleven, ranging from assault with a deadly weapon, to soliciting and a couple of breaking and entering charges.

He had clawed his way out of the gutter he'd been born in, his mother a fifteen-year-old runaway, and he had no intention whatsoever of ever going back to that kind of life. He was prepared to torture and kill anyone the boss asked him to, if it kept him out of the streets. He was well-versed in the art of extortion and coercion, and had also dabbled in kidnapping. He'd become known as a knee-breaker on the rough streets of D.C.

The boss was a complicated man, striving toward making the world a better place. He fought for what he believed in and accomplished feats that no other could, but little did the public know it had been bought with the threat of war or pain. The boss used his power and position to get what he wanted, all for the greater good, of course, and skirted the laws he vowed to uphold.

Sean never understood that sentiment. The world couldn't be changed, not really. He believed it to be a complete waste of time.

Hey, what do I know?

He just wanted to make money, and lots of it. He had a five-year plan, and at the end, he'd retire and live the life he should've always had. Nothing would get in the way of that.

The boss put down the phone and looked across the dark-stained heavy oak desk at him. The man was nervous, and Sean had never seen him look like that before. As a man of power and strength, he'd never appeared concerned by anything thrown at him. Always poised and calm, with a stiff upper lip and a backbone of pure steel. A man whose white collar upbringing showed in just about every movement he made. Sean knew he'd never had to *really* work for anything, everything pretty much handed to him on a silver fucking platter.

The boss had never starved because his mother had spent all their money on drugs instead of food, never had to watch his mother service roadies time and time again. The boss had gone to college, got himself a master's degree, and became a well-respected man high up on the food chain. Nothing ever changed. Born to one world, stay in that world. Well, not for Sean. He would not die a pauper with syphilis or some such disease. He would die surrounded by young hot chicks, hopefully in a hot tub at his own mansion.

He brought his thoughts back from his fantasy, and on to the matter at hand. A lot rode on the boss's next decision, and if he got caught it would be considered treason, and that would be the end of him. He would be destroying lives and making a lot of people sweat. Not an easy decision to make, even for a man like him.

Sean had no such qualms. That was the difference between him and the boss. He felt quite happy to do the dirty jobs, and not worry about the outcomes so long as he got paid for his troubles.

Not that the boss had clean hands. He had read somewhere that the boss had seen action in Vietnam. He had been wounded and walked away with a Medal of Honor and a Purple Heart. He was one tough son-of-a-bitch, that was for sure. He was like a cockroach, and could withstand any type of blast.

"So what about these men you have hired?" the boss asked, scrutinizing him closely.

"I did as you asked. Found two who are perfect. Great recommendations. They can do the job."

The boss's eyebrow rose, skepticism plain on his face. Annoyance flared. He'd worked hard, yet the boss questioned his competency. They'd worked together for several months and each time the boss had requested he carry out a certain assignment, he'd done so without comment or complaint. The boss looked down on him. No matter what he did, the boss remained unimpressed.

"And they fit *all* the requirements?" the boss pressed.

"Yes, boss." He contained the urge to shudder, hating being subservient to anyone.

It had taken time to find what the boss wanted, but the most important factor was that it couldn't lead back to Americans. If the boss's plan worked, no American could be blamed for the job.

Ivanov Consulting had the best reputation in the world of whispers and secrets, and could infiltrate the most complex computer programs. He was glad he'd found them.

Even so, it remained clear the boss thought he was better than Sean. Everyone thought they were above him. At least until they needed drugs, or a certain prostitute or mistress taken care of. Then he became their best friend. Once the job had been done, Sean Henry would be forgotten. Always.

Which was why he kept a detailed ledger of all transactions between them—and other members of high society—just in case any of them were stupid enough to sell him out.

He had to make sure everything went smoothly tomorrow. There was no room for error. What the boss proposed was risky to the both of them. He wasn't about to leave everything up to the old coot, no matter what power backed him.

He knew if the shit hit the fan, it would rain down hard, and he'd be on the bottom of the pile. He wouldn't go easily, though. No, he'd happily take half of D.C. down with him. Something the elite would soon learn, should they try to double cross him.

He might have been a bottom feeder, but he was also a smart one.

Chapter 4

Dmitry stepped out of the shower. The bathroom had filled with steam and the mirror above the basin was coated in condensation. He wiped away a section on the mirror with a towel, then shaved carefully. He dabbed on a small amount of cologne, careful not to overdo it. After brushing his teeth and gargling with mouthwash, he dressed in a crisp black suit and a sky blue shirt.

He wanted to make a good first and lasting impression on this client. He wasn't one for dressing in suits, except for a wedding or funeral, but he figured this would be the perfect opportunity to bring the suit out of the back of his closet and air it out. It had taken a dry clean to remove the moth ball scent from the fabric.

He gently ran a lint brush over his shoulders and combed his black hair to one side. His hair was so dark that sometimes it looked almost blue, and was in perfect contrast to his cool grey eyes. Satisfied he was ready, he left the bathroom and came face to face with a very intoxicated Ivan.

He wrinkled up his nose. "Dear God, what is that smell?"

Ivan stared back at him through bloodshot eyes, looking like road kill, and he didn't smell much better. His clothes were wrinkled and bore more than one unknown stain. His unshaved face made him look more like an escaped convict than a businessman, and he could barely stand, swaying slightly on his feet.

"Had a good time, did you?" Dmitry asked.

Ivan seemed to scrutinize him through a haze of alcohol. "Yeah, I did," he slurred as he tried to right himself. "Had myself a pretty little American girl."

Dmitry rolled his eyes. Same old Ivan. The man never changed, never grew up, and unfortunately never learned from his mistakes. "Hope she was over twenty-one. You ready to go?" he asked, knowing full well Ivan wasn't. The man's body probably consisted of around ninety percent alcohol.

"Give me a minute to freshen up," Ivan said, enunciating each word carefully like a child first learning to talk. He stumbled towards the bathroom, moving precariously side to side, and Dmitry wondered if he would have to call for an ambulance when Ivan stumbled into the stylish sparkling jade tiles that made up the four-star bathroom. His friend groaned, rubbing at his head as he closed the bathroom door.

When the shower turned on, Dmitry sank down heavily on the bed and resisted the urge to run his fingers through his carefully combed hair. He had a tendency to do that often when stressed or frustrated, and right now he was both. He slipped into his black loafers, which he'd spent the good part of an hour shining.

So much for first impressions.

He doubted Ivan had gotten any sleep last night. The man barely fired on all cylinders when he was sober. Dmitry wasn't too enthusiastic to see how the meeting would go, considering the situation. He only hoped Ivan would not get too riled up or take something the wrong way. He was always ready for a fight.

Twenty minutes later, Ivan returned from the bathroom a new man. He had shaved, although not too well, judging by all the pieces of bloodied toilet paper stuck to his face. He appeared semi-normal, a good thing for Ivan, and he wasn't going to get any better with time. He wore a dark chocolate suit which looked slightly wrinkled, and his mousey brown hair had been greased back.

He should have known this would happen. Ivan was a great man and a good friend, but he had no sense of decorum. He never knew when he should stop and always took several steps over the line. Dmitry had saved him many times, either from the clinker or an angry boyfriend of some woman he had been trying to pick up. He remembered one instance when he had gotten a shiner protecting Ivan from a beefy man who had taken offense to Ivan being too close to *his* woman.

Elena had not been impressed when she had to come down to the local MVD—Russia's police—in the middle of the night, or rather, the early morning. Her hair had been mussed from sleep and she had sported a deep scowl. He had to admit he had played the shiner for all it was worth to get out of the lecture Elena had on the tip on her tongue. She had used her connections with SVR to get him out of trouble and keep his record unblemished, and he'd made a point over the years to keep his nose clean. Something Elena certainly thanked him for.

Whatever he got caught doing would reflect on her. Dmitry knew Elena had an idea of the kinds of things he did when she was not around, and always pretended she didn't see or know anything. As an officer of the law, she was honor-bound to inform her bosses of the potential threat he posed to the security of the nation.

Dmitry stood and poured some hotel coffee into a Styrofoam cup and handed it to Ivan, who gratefully took it. Hopefully the caffeine would do him some good. Lord knew nothing else would.

"Are you going to be up for this, man?" he asked. "Would you prefer to stay here? I can go alone and close the deal for you."

Ivan shook his head then winced. "*Nyet.* All is good. Let's get this on the road, shall we?"

"All right. As long as you're sure." It would be a long day. Being hung-over would not improve his temperament.

Ivan picked up the keys to the Ford Focus and grinned at Dmitry. "Absolutely, man."

Dmitry instantly relieved Ivan of the keys and opened the hotel door for him.

Soon, they were in the car, heading east away from the hotel. Dmitry slid his black Ray-Ban sunglasses over the bridge of his nose to keep the sun out of his eyes as it rose over the buildings in preparation for a beautiful June day. The early morning traffic began to congest, and he was glad they were heading in a less busy direction.

Dmitry followed the GPS instructions, turning off Rhode Island Avenue and down a series of alleys in the Washington area of Langdon. The neighborhood was a world away from where he and Ivan had just come from. The streets and local businesses were filled with men who actually worked for a living, trying to keep their families afloat. Those who came home at night smelling of hard work and carried layers of dirt and grease on their bodies.

He drove past a series of warehouses, automotive repair shops, and storage companies before coming to a stop outside a single level structure. The building looked rather deserted for a place of business. He glanced about the street, double checking that he had the correct address.

He did.

Together, he and Ivan walked toward the door of the warehouse. Ivan knocked, the sound almost clanging against the thin metal. Someone opened the door almost immediately, and they were met by a tall man dressed in a suit. He looked at them both before stepping aside allowing them to enter the building.

If he thought Ivan's suit was bad, he wasn't sure how to describe the monstrosity this man wore. While the suit had been pressed, it gave off a subtle cheap look, and he guessed the man had only just recently purchased it, most likely for the meeting that was about to start. The suit had pinstripes down the length of the maroon fabric, and did nothing for his features, making him look like someone out of an Al Capone film, only with a smaller budget.

This American undoubtedly lacked taste, that much was clear.

Behind the not so well-dressed man stood another. This one did not try to disguise himself as anything other than what he was. The large man, his long oily ponytail hanging down his back, had to be hired muscle.

"Ivan Anisimov and Dmitry Ivanov?" the first man asked, his brown hair an inch too long for big business. "Stephen Hosking. We spoke on the phone." He extended his arm, and Ivan shook his hand, followed by Dmitry.

He noted the man's calloused palms and slightly dirty fingernails. He was accustomed to hard work. He frowned. Not the type to sit behind a desk all day. He glanced about the almost empty warehouse before turning back to his client, noting the wooden desk complete with a chair and a state-of-the-art computer system behind him, the only item which looked at odds to its surroundings.

"We're a relatively new company," the first man—Stephen—stated, once he noticed Dmitry take in their surroundings. "Still in the start-up phase, which is why we want you here. We're interested in getting our entire system computerized, to be used autonomously. To lessen the supervision required."

It sounded like something a lot of small time companies wanted, to limit the amount of employees they would need to pay. Especially in today's economy and recession, a dollar saved is always best.

"Sounds doable." His gaze swept the large, empty warehouse. Nothing had changed; he hadn't missed anything since looking around a moment ago. A prickle of unease raced down his back.

His attention moved to the muscle, whose expression gave nothing away. He looked fierce, and Dmitry doubted it was an act, because he seemed like the type who chewed on nails for breakfast. He crossed his large, thick arms across his chest, causing his muscles to plump. If Dmitry hadn't been Russian, he might have been scared or at least intimidated, but men like that grew on trees where he came from.

He shot Ivan a look as he and the client discussed the logistics company, noticing his friend's manner appeared relaxed. Ivan didn't seem worried about the situation. Dmitry started toward the computer, pushing aside his concerns and settled into a comfortable position in the chair, in front of the computer, while Ivan hung back.

"What kind of traffic are you looking at and how would you like this to be structured?" he asked as he began typing on the keyboard. He frowned when he saw how advanced—and expensive—the system was and knew immediately no start-up company could afford such an expenditure this early on. Not unless the company needed to hide sensitive information. Just what type of import and export business was the client running? His mind immediately went to drugs.

His stomach knotted, his concerns once again taking precedence, the feeling of impending doom washing over him that he couldn't shake. He could no longer ignore his discomfort. The client's phone beeped and the man glanced down and read the screen, his face changing in a heartbeat. He wondered what the message said. He and Ivan shared a glance.

"I believe, Mr. Ivanov, there has been a misunderstanding," Stephen began, tucking the phone back into his pocket. "I regret the misleading circumstances of your being here, but what I want is rather sensitive, and I could hardly advertise for such a thing. I want you to locate something for me. I am prepared to pay handsomely for it."

Dmitry's face darkened and he tensed, ready for possible attack. An unconscious reaction, which came from growing up in Moscow. Anger bubbled to the surface. He didn't like being played, especially as a fool. He'd accepted the job, wanting their business to succeed. He should've investigated his new client better instead of being blinded by money and prestige. He'd been careless.

Had the contents of the message the American received been a verification of his identity and Ivan's? It would explain why the client had suddenly lost all pretense. The reasons why such a measure had been required made him worry, his blood chilling at the implications.

"Not everything is for sale," he replied simply and truthfully. "I certainly am not."

He stood, only able to guess what the man wanted him to do. There were only a few things one could not advertise for, and he wasn't about to do something illegal for a man who misrepresented himself and his needs. He especially didn't like to be fucked about, and he wasn't even sure the man had given him his real name. He made his way toward Ivan.

"Wait," Stephen said. He held up his hands in surrender. "I apologize. Please stay."

Dmitry glanced over at Ivan, who shrugged, appearing perplexed. He turned to the American, preparing to hear him out. He would rather not waste the trip. So what if it was not quite the job he had been expecting? He could be flexible, depending on what the job entailed.

"What is it you want us to do *exactly*?" Dmitry asked.

He wouldn't make promises. He was a man of principal and integrity. He may not be the Russian Federation's man of the year, but there were certain things he would not do. Compromising innocent people was one of them. In fact, it was right up on the top of his list. He'd spent many nights knee-deep in illegal activities, so he wasn't a saint, but his actions had never been for personal or even monetary gain. He just liked seeing if he could penetrate the most elaborate security systems in the world. He soon discovered he could and did so often.

The client produced a piece of paper from his chest pocket, and handed it to Dmitry. He took the scrap of paper from him and viewed it. His stomach clenched as he took in the IP address.

Jesus fucking Christ.

31

It became clear he and Ivan were in deep shit. If they didn't watch themselves, they'd be buried in it. The IP was a government standard address; he knew the sequence of numbers well. The American couldn't possibly want him to bypass a government firewall. He would be fucking crazy if he did.

"There's been a mistake," he said. "This is government. That most certainly wasn't our deal."

He waved the piece of paper in front of him, knowing things were going south fast. While he liked to think of himself as a grey hat—a person who sometimes crossed the line between legal and illegal—he knew well enough to let sleeping dogs lie, and to never mess with federal governments. Particularly the Americans. If there had ever been a nation he didn't want to fuck over, it was them. Piss them off, and he'd have an enemy for life. He didn't want to have a satellite aimed on him until a squadron could take him out.

"Well, I'm changing the deal," the American declared, oblivious to the repercussions. Or he simply didn't care.

Which made him worry all the more.

"Even I'm smart enough to know it's stupid to fuck with the American government," Dmitry replied. "It's a good way to end up dead or have yourself and your family under surveillance for the next century. You Americans are not so forgiving as you let on to be."

The American produced a Desert Eagle from the waistband of his pants and had it pointed at Ivan before Dmitry could blink. His hand remained steady as he held the heavy gun, obviously familiar with the weapon. Dmitry realized too late he'd been right. The man was not a businessman, at least not the type he'd been expecting. He knew the rough side of living, and it showed clearly now that he wasn't trying to repress it.

"If you don't do as I ask, your friend here dies," he said, his voice cold and hard.

Dmitry held up his hands, not wanting the hot-headed American to get wound up and accidentally shoot Ivan. "Calm down. This won't get you anywhere."

The man's cool gaze flicked over him. "I seriously doubt that. In my experience, I rarely get any objections after I bring out my big gun."

Ivan rolled his eyes in a gesture Dmitry recognized. His friend had become unimpressed and bored. Not good. Ivan could barely keep his mouth shut at the best of times, though he understood how he felt; it was hard to take the theatrics seriously.

"Where we come from, there are some *actual* scary mother-fuckers, not some two-bit wannabes like you," Ivan said, his tone contemptuous.

Dmitry closed his eyes and counted to ten, letting his breath out slowly, trying to remain calm. It wasn't working. His blood pressure shot through the roof and he could feel the tension in his muscles.

Way to open your mouth, Ivan. Talk about hot headed.

The American would surely shoot them just to prove the length of his manhood.

"Ivan," Dmitry whispered, shaking his head slightly when his friend turned to look at him. Ivan, a man who could sell snow cones in the middle of a Russian winter, didn't have much diplomacy when it came to these types of situations. Dmitry didn't want him to say anything that could be regretted later.

"I have no time to mess around. One of you are going to get me what I want. I don't care who or how, just fucking do it."

"I'd tell you to get fucked but I don't think it will do any good," Ivan retorted. He took a stance of nonchalance, just a normal day for him.

The American poised his index finger on the trigger, tightening his grip, and a second later, a loud bang resounded. Blindsided, not expecting the man to follow through, he watched in horror, powerless to intercede, as Ivan crumpled to the floor. Blood stained his shirt, the crimson liquid bubbling and running out of the neat round bullet hole in his chest.

Chapter 5

"Ivan," Dmitry shouted, dropping to his knees beside his best friend. Lifting Ivan's head away from the hard floor, he pressed his palm to the wound in hopes of slowing the blood loss.

Ivan struggled to breathe, each attempt quick and uneasy. Tears gathered in Dmitry's eyes, watching helplessly as his friend of over twenty years bled out onto the dusty concrete floor of the warehouse, the fluid seeping between his fingers.

He willed Ivan to live, praying, offering everything from his health to his first born child. He and Ivan had been through a lot together, were brothers in every way except blood, and here he was about to lose him.

This cannot be happening.

They were here for a job, just an easy reprogram. They had been so happy with their new business venture, ecstatic when they'd been offered the job in the States. Ivan had called it their adventure, and here he was about to die without really living it.

Dmitry thought back to that morning, when he

had asked Ivan if he'd wanted to stay at the hotel. If he had, none of this would be happening. He shook his head to clear his errant thoughts. He couldn't change what had happened, or go back in time to alter it. Tears rained down his cheeks, yet he barely noticed. His entire consciousness remained on the man before him, his friend and confidant. The man who had gotten him into trouble time and time again. This time, it was he who had gotten Ivan into trouble. It was his fault Ivan was here, his fault he'd taken the bullet.

His life dimmed. A range of emotions he generally kept bottled up ran hotly through his body. Anger. Fear. Rage. Hopelessness. He begged and prayed, threatened and promised, but Ivan's blood continued to spill from his body. His skin felt cool to the touch while perspiration beaded on his forehead. His friend shook uncontrollably and Dmitry knew it wouldn't be long now.

"Promise me you'll get the *sraka,* Dmitry," Ivan gasped, fighting for breath. A lone crimson trail escaped the side of his mouth and ran down his jaw.

He didn't bother lying to Ivan, telling him it would be all right. It couldn't be. He could only do his best to fulfill his friend's last wish, and Dmitry planned to make the asshole responsible pay for his crime. Provided he himself was alive to do so.

He nodded. "I promise."

With one last shuddering breath, Ivan's eyes became glassy, staring sightlessly up at him. He slumped over, barely holding back a howl of anguish. He knew there was nothing he could've done. Even had he been free to go—which was impossible now—he would never have made it to a hospital in time. The American had been accurate with his shot, fully intending to kill.

The evil man didn't even bat an eyelash. He turned the gun on Dmitry as he slowly rose to his feet. Dmitry kept his hands where they were, visible to the man wielding the weapon. He didn't want to annoy the American any more than he already had and wanted the chance to walk away from this, even though he would do so without his best friend. He didn't think his odds were great. He knew he was a dead man walking, and as soon as he gave the man what he wanted, he would end up just like Ivan.

"All that could have been avoided," the suit told him. "Now do as I ask or you'll be joining your friend."

Dmitry silently prayed he would get out of this alive. Nothing would work out now that his best friend was dead at the hands of a deranged sociopath, but maybe Dmitry could live. He sent the American a glare, wanting so much to destroy the man who'd shot and killed Ivan.

Now is not the time. He was unarmed and outnumbered. Somewhere deep inside him, an almost animalistic urge roared, a burning rage to fight. He tampered down his emotions, vowing to live to fight another day, pushing all irrelevant feelings aside, blinking away the tears gathering in his eyes. Now was not the time to fall apart. There would be plenty of time for that later. Now was the time to use his brain.

He sat down at the chair by the desk and poised his fingers over the keyboard, waiting for instructions from the American. He tried not to think of Ivan lying dead only a few feet away. He tried to block out the awareness of the weapon trained on him, the same gun used to kill his friend. He could feel the damp sheen of nervous sweat coating his back and forehead and a chill ran down the length of his spine.

The American returned the piece of paper to him. He stared at the damning numbers and began to type. His fingers barely touched the keys as he blindly typed in a series of commands. He copied the IP address into the command box and soon found himself at the Department of Defense's mainframe. He sucked in a deep breath.

Oh shit. The Pentagon. Great, just fucking fantastic. Of all the government agencies to hack, they had to choose DoD.

He bypassed the firewall in mere seconds. For the Pentagon, their security was not at all what it should have been. The firewall had been designed to keep hackers out. While it was strong and barred most, he found himself well past the firewall and now battling the antivirus software as he uploaded his own brand of DoS—a Denial of Service—which effectively bombarded the mainframe with external communications, rendering the system slow and non-responsive, allowing him unlimited access.

He found the government's network-based intrusion-detection system laughable. He could write a better program in his sleep. Infiltrating the network was almost not worth his time, because any fool could do the job. He sure could show them a thing or two about security, and wondered once again why the American felt the need to hire an overseas team when a local one could have served just as well.

The answers that came to him made him sweat all the more. He certainly wasn't liking any of the reasons that floated about his head. He needed a plan—a smart plan—and he needed it now. He didn't have the luxury of believing he would get out of this warehouse alive, even though he hoped. He knew too much.

He added another set of commands. On a normal day, had his friend not just been murdered, and had he been doing this of his own free will, he would have enjoyed himself. Instead, he felt edgy and afraid, sensing the crosshairs of the gun. No matter what happened in the next hour, his life would be over. Even if he happened to get away, he would be forced to hide for the rest of his life. Every keystroke was another nail in his coffin.

"How long is this going to take?" the American demanded.

Had Rome been taken in a day? *Have some fucking patience.*

"Even baking a cake takes forty minutes," he replied, glancing at the hand holding the gun. "Also, I'm not used to working while I have a gun pointed at me."

The American lowered his weapon, but didn't holster it. "Hurry up about it," he snapped, then paced back and forth behind him.

Dmitry turned his attention back to the black command box hovering in the top left hand corner of his screen, above the Department of Defense's logo, and ignored his surroundings.

He opened the file marked System Administrator and created a new persona. He named it GreyHat01, the general ID he had for adding users. It kept things simple. He always knew what to look for when he needed to go back to wipe out his tracks. While this was his trademark, he wasn't stupid enough to leave it where it could be found and traced back to him. If he ever got caught, he'd rather not be linked to all of his jobs.

Using his new status as an administrator, he uploaded a ghost—which if the DoD's antivirus or system watcher detected the intrusion, would install a new ghost in milliseconds after the previous one had been deleted or flagged. The ghost's job was to collect the information required in the quickest time possible. While he would normally upload his own brand of spyware, he didn't have the timeframe needed. Spyware collected bits of information over a period of time, and due to the fact that the American stood agitated behind him, Dmitry didn't think he had minutes let alone hours or even days, so he didn't bother.

He sat back in his chair and looked over his shoulder at the man. "I'm in. What is it you need?"

The American smirked. "There's a file imbedded somewhere deep in the system, marked by the name Sundown. I want you to retrieve the data. That's it."

Dmitry nodded and began to locate the ominous file. After three minutes of searching through the congestion of files on the server, he came across the file hidden amongst the yearly budget and staff directory. He had no idea what it could be, and had no time to flick through it, but he knew if the man behind him would kill for it, it had to be something pretty damn important.

He was sure he wouldn't like the reason they wanted Sundown. An innocuous name, but the DoD liked giving their missions and contacts ridiculous code words. As if it would somehow make them feel better when Operation Wild Rider killed hundreds of innocent civilians so one bad guy would be taken out. He didn't understand that type of logic, even as an extremely logical man.

He was also far from stupid. The moment the file finished downloading, he would be dead, lying next to Ivan while the American absconded with the mysterious file. He would most likely be blamed for the theft of Sundown, his name forever associated with terrorism. He thought about Elena and how it would affect her. She would be heartbroken to lose him, and he wondered if she would survive such a blow. He knew she would never accept that he would do such a thing and she would risk death trying to prove his innocence, just as she had when she'd searched for the truth about Nikolai.

He couldn't allow that. His sister had been through enough. He couldn't let her deal with his death on top of everything else. With renewed resolve not to die today, he worked on his plan to escape unscathed. It wasn't a very good plan, certainly not his best, but he was under extreme pressure and time restraints. He knew once he did what he was about to do, he would have a giant red target painted on his ass. But he would not let the scum bags get away with it.

41

He sent his ghost to the file, adding extra commands as he did so. He could feel the countdown begin as he pressed the enter button. He knew he had ten minutes to get the hell out of there, and he watched the dialog box appear in the center of the screen as the contents of the Sundown file began transferring to the hard drive of the computer he was using. He added more commands, praying the man wielding the gun didn't notice as he continued to work. He worked faster, watching the transfer box closely as the time passed. The file was copying at amazing speed, currently at sixty-five percent. It would not be much longer now. He finished entering his commands and sat back, waiting, watching for his moment to act.

The blue horizontal line filled up the box, indicating that it had reached one hundred percent. The computer beeped, informing them the transfer had completed. Dmitry stepped away from the computer, almost overwhelmed by a sense of joy at being finished with the task. He blinked and the feeling was gone, things slipping into motion. He watched the American carefully, determining the moves he would make when he discovered what Dmitry had done.

He backed up, standing beside Ivan's body, then glanced down at his friend once more, sending up a silent prayer for his soul. He added an apology for not being able to save him. It certainly wasn't the way a man like Ivan would have chosen to go out. Dmitry imagined something more along the lines of an epic battle over a woman not worth anybody's time. He'd been wrong. Now he had to leave his friend here with his killer. Who knew what would happen to his body. He would make things right, even if it was the last thing he did. Hopefully, that would not be the case.

While he'd been working, he'd ignored the muscle who stood nearby. Now, he watched him out the corner of his eye as he edged nearer to the door. He didn't want to fight the man who easily outweighed him by thirty pounds.

"Perfect," Ivan's murderer intoned, viewing the information available on the screen. He looked positively gleeful.

It made Dmitry feel sick. This bastard was up to no good with that information. If only he'd had a chance to review the material inside the file. He might know what he was dealing with, and who he might be up against. Unfortunately, he had to work with what he had. Which wasn't much. Heat from the hired muscle's body burned his skin as the man flanked him. Once again, he began to get the sensation that he was done for and rapidly considered his options.

"Congratulations, Mr. Ivanov." The American brought the sight of the gun in line with Dmitry's chest.

He took a step back, bumping into the bulky arm of the body builder. His heart pounded guiltily in his chest, his blood cool as he looked down the barrel of the weapon. A drop of perspiration slid down his spine, and he shivered in response. There was nothing like the feeling of looking at the face of death with both eyes open. It somehow made him feel alive.

The American's finger moved to the trigger.

Come on, come on. Any time now.

He glanced at the computer just as it started beeping loudly, like a heart monitor during a cardiac arrest. The American turned on his heel, seeking out the noise, and looked at the computer as the Department of Defense's intruder alert symbol and alarm appeared on the screen, flashing its warning:

"You are in a restricted area. Remove yourself at once. Your connection is being traced."

"What the fuck," the American shouted, watching the recently downloaded file dispersing, sending pieces of itself across the globe. "No." He screamed, then shot to the keyboard and began typing as if he could stop it.

Dmitry spun around, landing a fist hard into the muscle man's firm stomach. His hand stung as if he'd punched granite, and had he not known better, he would've sworn that every bone in his hand had shattered from the impact. He bit off a curse, his hand throbbing, and pushed away the pain the best he could.

The hired muscle grabbed him hard by the throat, lifting him several inches off the floor. The man's dirty fingernails dug into his skin, Dmitry's legs dangling in the air as he caught hold of the arm that suspended him in an attempt to relieve some of the pressure. His lungs burned, and his vision started to dim, the darkness calling to him.

He kicked as hard as he could, his assault inadequate against a man of his opponent's bulk. He could feel the force against his trachea and struggled to breathe. Another minute or two and he'd be unconscious, and then he really would be fucked. He removed his hands from his attacker's arms and moved them to the man's face, ignoring the urge to shudder as he pressed his thumbs firmly down on the corneas, straining the moist eyeballs.

He sensed the beast trying to ignore the pain as he squeezed Dmitry's neck harder in return. Darkness blurred the edges of his sight. He wouldn't last much longer.

He dug his thumbs deeper into the sockets. He ignored the sensation of touching slippery eyeballs and concentrated on inflicting as much pain as possible. He bent his head back as far as he could before jerking it forward fast, head-butting the man hard enough to daze the both of them. Stars burst in his vision and a massive headache started pounding. The man dropped him to his feet, and Dmitry stumbled as he tried to regain his equilibrium. He sucked in deep breaths as the attacker turned his immediate attention to himself.

The beeping of the security alarm scared him just as much as the two men. He knew they would have company soon, and not the pleasant kind. There was no reason to stick around. He would retrieve the data at a later date. Right now, it was safe, away from the likes of the American. He headed for the exit, praying the man remained occupied and more worried about the flashing screen deleting the file and the piercing siren than he was about Dmitry.

***

Sean tried in vain to stop the file from sending. He had never been a wiz at the computer, hating them and the world's reliance on them. They helped him with his business, and because of that he was thankful and semi-tolerant, but that's all. He spun around to face the fucking Russian, ready to put a bullet into the useless bastard's body. The man had such good references, but from the very first had been a royal pain in his ass. He thought it would have been easy to pay the man for the job, but as it turned out the commie prick had principals.

Such a useless trait in today's world.

He'd had high hopes for the Russian. He and his partner had been the perfect fall guys. With Ivanov's history of hacking and Anisimov's criminal record, no jury in the country would ever believe them innocent. Killing Ivan had been a means to an end—to force Ivanov's hand. But again the Russian had defied him. Now he had to regroup, think of a new plan.

The boss wouldn't be pleased he had failed, even more so now that Sundown had been handed to the public, dispersed all over the world. It would be even harder to retrieve from around the globe.

Truthfully, he preferred Anisimov dead. In his experience, dead men tell no tales and therefore cast no suspicion to him. Desire to shoot Ivanov filled him. He didn't tolerate being made to feel inept and stupid and the Russian had done both. For now, the bastard would stay alive…at least until he'd gotten what he wanted. He needed him to retrieve

Sundown. He would simply need to find a better bargaining piece, one the Russian valued more than own life. When he had the file in his possession once more, Ivanov would suffer painfully at his hands.

Narrowing his eyes, he turned and found the Russian running toward the exit. Rage overcame him, his vision reddening. He tried to bite back the searing anger but he'd gone way past that. Hatred for Ivanov fueled him, his blood boiling as he watched the one man who dared fuck with him headed for freedom.

Without thought beyond his rage, he raised the gun, barely feeling the weight of his weapon as he aimed it at the Russian. It was more like an extended part of him than an inanimate object. He had no issues killing anyone, least of all the smug bastard who'd ruined his entire operation. His hand, once calm and steady, now trembled with anger as he decompressed the trigger. He felt the powerful weapon discharge, recoiling, and only familiarity kept the barrel pointed at his prey and not at the ceiling.

Chapter 6

Dmitry felt something like a bee sting on his upper arm as the sound of a bullet exiting the chamber filled the room. He gritted his teeth against the sharp pain, each second causing increasing discomfort. He swore eloquently, knowing he'd been shot but he couldn't afford to slow down. If he stopped or slowed now he was a dead man. Apparently, the American had finished working with him.

He applied pressure against the wound with his uninjured hand as he continued running. He detected the warm sticky liquid beneath his palm, needing to fix himself up as soon as possible. A hospital was out of the question. Every gunshot wound was reported to the police and he couldn't risk that.

He would be extremely easy to trace once he got into the system or in police custody. As a Russian citizen, he didn't have the appropriate medical insurance required for most American hospitals. Not that he couldn't afford to pay any of the fees, it would just take time to internationally transfer the funds. Once again, he would be stuck here while waiting for the money to clear.

He caught hold of the door to the street and just managed to slip through the opening when he heard another booming *pop* sound and then the clang of metal hitting another source of metal. He barely glanced back. He didn't need to know just how close he had been to copping another bullet. He took off at a fast speed for the rental car without another thought.

Holy shit, what the fuck have I gotten involved in?

The American had no compunctions about murder. If he caught him, he might torture him first, get him to recover Sundown before killing him. His death would tie up loose ends—just another tourist found dead. A poor unfortunate victim of a mugging.

He needed to think, regroup. To come back bigger and better, stronger and clear minded. He would make the bastards pay for what they'd done to Ivan and what they were trying to do to him, but first he needed to be anywhere but here. Especially when the Department of Defense arrived.

He knew he was in deep trouble, and he wouldn't be able to get out on his own. He needed help and lots of it. He had just hacked the goddamn Pentagon—a criminal offense, a one way ticket to sunny Gitmo. The consulate was out. Once they learned who he was, he'd merely be trading one prison for another. He knew of only one person who could possibly do anything. If he had any chance of getting out of this alive, without doing jail time, he had to seek out the big guns. The one man who could understand his predicament. After all, he'd been through the exact same thing not that long ago. However, it would cause some major issues.

Oh, well. He was up shit creek, and Lucas was the only one who could hand him a paddle. *Sorry, Elena. My ass comes before your heart.*

***

Sean spun around, breathing heavily. The Russian fucker had gotten away, making his job all the more difficult. Now he'd have to hunt down the bastard and kill him. He didn't have time for this, but he couldn't risk sending anyone else to do the job. He needed to make sure it got done, that it couldn't come back to bite him in the ass. There was no way the boss would accept any loose ends or failures on his part, and he sure as hell didn't want to disappoint the boss. He couldn't afford to lose the credibility he had worked so hard to make, for it to be washed down the drain with this one fuck-up.

He pulled out the acid bottle from a briefcase hidden beside the desk and squeezed the bottle hard, the liquid contents moving through the straw and entering through the DVD crevice. Acid flowed down towards the computer's internal hardware. He heard the sizzling as it ate away at the memory and hard drive, and he watched as the steam escaped through the air holes of the computer box. His clean up here was done, ensuring the Feds wouldn't find any trace of him in the warehouse, which had been leased under a dummy corporation that would lead nowhere.

He smiled. Something had finally gone in his favor. There was no way to recover the data now, the acid having done its job. The information was gone, without a trace. Not even the tech guys within the alphabet agencies were that good.

Now he had some explaining to do to his boss, and he wasn't looking forward to that conversation. The boss wouldn't be impressed, and would once again look at him like an incompetent idiot. He took a deep breath before the anger at the Russian could overrule his better judgment. He admitted he'd lost his cool earlier and he'd made a mistake shooting at the bastard, but luckily he hadn't killed him. He had a moment of pleasure as he thought how he would enjoy the task once he got his hands on the commie. Yes, he'd make sure Ivanov felt every ounce of frustration he'd gone through right before he put a bullet in the man's head.

Chapter 7

Secretary of Defense Walter Mann glanced about his office on the west side of the Pentagon as the alarm shrilled. He stood and moved to the doorway. His office overlooked the open area workspace, which was full of activity. Men and women in navy blue pressed uniforms and formal suits moved quickly about the room. Each having their own job to do in such an event. The tech teams were each manning their stations. The sound of dexterous fingertips gliding almost sensuously over individual keyboards echoed throughout the room. The numerous techs' faces were masks of concentration and concern as they worked hard.

Movement in his peripheral vision had him turning to his second in command. Captain Moore moved speedily towards him, a look of apprehension on his usually composed face. They had worked together for over five years, and had served together for another ten. They each knew the other's temperaments and moods well. Moore, for one, was as straitlaced as they came. Nothing ever seemed to faze him or ruffle his feathers—until now. Moore stopped before him and took a deep breath, obviously preparing himself to report the news.

Apprehension grew and cool sweat broke out on his skin as he waited. The gruff looking captain met his eyes. "Sir, I regret to inform you we just had a security breach of our internal systems."

While he had prepared himself for the news, perhaps another war outbreak, he was floored. Never once in his tenure, or to his knowledge, his predecessor's time, had there ever been a successful breach of the Pentagon. Who would be stupid enough—or desperate enough—to hack into the DoD? This was a fuck-up of epic proportions. How had they gotten in?

The Department of Defense had state of the art protection against this type of infiltration. It was embarrassing to say the least and he had to admit he wasn't looking forward to explaining this to the White House. He only prayed the perpetrator kept quiet about the hack otherwise they'll have every Tom, Dick, and Harry taking shots at them.

"How far did they get in and what did they do?" he asked, holding his breath. His mind ran through several scenarios, each one worse than the last.

Captain Moore swallowed nervously, the action catching his sharp eye, worrying him even more. If the intrusion had been enough to make the captain nervous—someone who'd seen action amidst raining bullets, flying missiles and injured serviceman—he wondered just how bad things were. *What the hell did they get? Launch codes?*

The exact co-ordinates of the Nevada test site?

"The intruder made it into the mainframe, sir. Deep inside. We managed to trace his movements, although it was quite difficult. We're certainly dealing with a professional, no doubt about that. He went directly to an obscure file named Sundown. There were no signs of anything else being compromised, sir. The man knew what he was looking for."

He felt the blood drain from his face, immediately light headed. He grabbed hold of the doorframe to keep himself up, his legs no longer able to hold up his weight.

Sundown. Of all the files it could have been. Holy fuck.

The only thing worse was being unaware of what the bastard who hacked the file intended to do with it. They would be walking around blind until they knew whether a ransom demand would be made, or whether the file would be placed on the black market. He would have to make sure he had several men monitoring all communications searching for any reference of the file. He would also need to liaise with the NSA to make use of their super computer. If there was ever a time for inter-agency support, it had to be now.

"Do we have anything on the hacker?"

Moore nodded. "Yes, sir. We traced his IP and came up with an address in Langdon. He was one hell of a cocky son-of-a-bitch. He didn't attempt anything at all to cover his tracks."

He gave the orders to prepare, had his men pack for the occasion, decked out in Kevlar with rifles and handguns at the ready. He wasn't about to let this fucker go. He wanted to have a one on one with the bastard. He had no patience when it came to those who endangered the country he loved so dearly.

Twenty minutes later, he was standing in the almost empty warehouse looking down at a recently deceased man. He had already called for the city medical examiner and was now waiting on the older man to make his way across town to join him. His men were surrounding him, collecting evidence and securing the area. The warehouse had been abandoned except for one lone table, a computer placed upon it. He could smell the faint scent of acid and burned electronics in the air, knowing they were too late. Whatever secrets the computer could've revealed were now destroyed. Even he knew they would be hard pressed to retrieve any data from the hard drive.

Acid worked quickly and it worked well, destroying everything in its path. The perpetrator was long gone and wouldn't be back, by the looks of the computer and the body on the floor. He was still in the process of getting the name on the warehouse's lease, but it proved difficult. The last report he'd received from the tech guys back at the Pentagon was that the name of the company was a fake, nothing more than a front.

He watched as Captain Moore went down on one knee, his back straight as a board, years of military training ingrained into every fiber of his being so that every movement he made was unconscious. Both he and Moore had signed up during the same month, went on to complete their training together, and learned to trust the other completely with their lives. When he had been promoted to Secretary of Defense, Moore had been his first and only choice as second in command. The man knew his job and did it well, always keeping up with his fitness regime—even after leaving the military life— running three miles in the morning before doing one hundred push-ups and another hundred sit-ups.

Moore methodically searched the dead man's pockets, allowing for no mistakes or missing any key piece of evidence. He brought out a wallet and maroon passport and handed them to him. Walter immediately flipped the passport open to the particulars page and looked down at the photo and name.

This just keeps getting better and better.

"Ivan Mikhailovich Anisimov," he read out loud. He shook his head. A fucking Russian citizen—the last thing he needed. There was nothing worse than having an international crisis on their hands. Things were precarious between the States and the Russian Federation, and this situation wouldn't improve matters. He turned around and waved his hand in the air, signaling to his men to wrap up. He had calls to make, the first being to the White House to report the incident. The second would be to the Russian Consulate. They all needed to agree to a course of action now before the situation had a chance to escalate. A lot of lives hung in the balance of their decisions.

He exited the warehouse, happy to be away from the scent of death. He watched as the medical examiner stepped out of his van and started over. Walter had no idea how the man could be around dead bodies all the time. He'd seen his fair share during his tours overseas. He just never liked being reminded that life was precious and death lurked around every corner.

Chapter 8

Lucas Gates raised his right arm. He held his weapon steady as he shot off all the rounds in his clip. Focused, his mind clear as he aimed at the paper target at the end of the firing range. He felt his cell phone vibrate against his hip where it was attached to his belt. He released the empty magazine and holstered his weapon, then stepped out of the firing booth, unsnapped his cell, and viewed the caller ID.

'Fitzgibbon.'

James Fitzgibbon was his boss, the man who'd taken on the rough D.C. cop Lucas had once been, and made him the agent *and* man he was today. He owed a lot to Jim and refused any promotion that came his way that took him from under Special Agent in Charge Fitzgibbon. Not only did he owe Jim, he revered the older agent who had become a living legend. Jim was also the only one who would put up with his shit, as he often skated over the line in pursuit of justice which had gotten him into trouble more times than he could count.

Once he was out of the firing range where the sound of gunshots were muffled through the drywall, he returned the call. Fitzgibbon was short and to the point when he answered, "Get your ass to my office now."

Ten minutes later, Lucas opened the door to SAC Fitzgibbon's office. The space was bland even by government standards and his boss hadn't done anything to add life to the place in which he spent most of his time. The cream walls were bare and matched the filing cabinet, and the dark grey carpet was clean but worn in places. The furnishings were minimal yet suited the man he knew didn't give a fig about interior design. He stepped further into the office, the faint drone of the air conditioner filling the silence as it pumped out semi-cool air.

Jim sat behind his desk, a sour look on his face. Lucas wondered briefly as to what he'd done wrong. There wasn't anything recent that he could think of. But then again, the look could also be attributed to the ulcers burning a hole through his stomach lining. Jim's sweet wife Maggie continually nagged him to go see a doctor. Lucas had always thought Maggie was too good for the old bastard. She put up with a hell of a lot being his wife—the long nights, the secrets. Not many women would stay married to a man whose life remained somewhat a mystery.

"What's up, Jim?"

Fitzgibbon glared at him, his brow pinched into a frown. "Nothing you're going to like, I guarantee it."

Lucas took one of the two visitor chairs opposite

Fitzgibbon and waited.

"I just got a call from DoD," Jim continued once Lucas had settled down. "It seems they have a problem. They were hacked earlier this morning and when they went to the location, they found a DB. They sent me photos of the crime scene."

Fitzgibbon clicked his mouse a few times before adjusting his computer monitor to allow Lucas to see. The photos were of a warehouse in a blue collar neighborhood. He thought he recognized the structure as one of the many in Langdon. Inside the warehouse was a lone computer, the system expensive. Something a professional high class hacker would use and apparently managed to infiltrate the Pentagon's mainframe with. He took in the shots of the dismantled computer as the DoD's tech people tried to save the data. The dead body shot appeared next. One shot to the chest. No defensive wounds and no visible signs of torture. As far as he could see from the pictures, it was a clean, professional kill.

"If he was the hacker, he wasn't working alone," Jim said.

Lucas nodded. Whoever the man had been working with, the partnership hadn't end well.

"Do we know who he was?" Lucas asked, leaning forward to get a better look at the victim.

This was not CIA warranted—NSA maybe, FBI most surely. He waited, calm.

"Passport was in his left pocket. Belonged to an Ivan Mikhailovich Anisimov. The medical examiner identified the dead body as Anisimov at the scene. He arrived in the country late last night."

Lucas looked at Fitzgibbon, still waiting. Dread built inside him. He could see the truth plain as day on his face. He wanted to deny it with his last breath. Lucas closed his eyes and silently prayed.

Please be a Ukrainian or Latvian anything but Russian. His wishes were ignored.

"Anisimov was a Russian citizen."

Lucas nodded, expecting it. By the look on Fitzgibbon's face, he'd known what Lucas's reaction to the news would be. He also got the sense that wasn't all.

"I have his flight manifest here, faxed over by DoD." He handed him the fax. "Check out who Anisimov was sitting beside."

Lucas's stomach clenched, automatically preparing for bad news. He looked down at the piece of paper in his hands of Rossiya Airlines Flight A256. He found Ivan Anisimov's name easily enough. He had sat in seat J21. J22 however held a name he was well familiar with—Dmitry Ivanov. He prayed it was a different man. The name Dmitry Ivanov was as common in Russia as John Smith was in America.

He looked at Fitzgibbon, who shook his head. "Sorry, Lucas, checked it out already with immigration. They sent over his passport information. He's one and the same."

Shit. What the hell have you gotten yourself into, Dmitry?

The man was his friend, and Lucas knew he never would have voluntarily tried to infiltrate the Pentagon, not without a damn good reason.

Elena wouldn't like this. The thought of her

warmed his blood. It had been eighteen months since he had last seen her, and in that time, he'd hoped she would have learned to love him.

He and Elena had struggled with their newly developing feelings while fighting to stay alive, trying to find the killer of her late husband, and he had told her he would wait until she was ready. He was still waiting.

Her brother Dmitry worked in the private sector, but was never known to actively infiltrate government bodies, particularly foreign governments. It just wasn't like him. He used his genius to create security programs, not to steal or create terror by crashing sites and causing mischief. Dmitry well understood the power he had, and was always cautious.

"That could mean just about anything," Lucas said, rushing to his friend's defense. "Just because they sat next to each other doesn't necessarily mean they were traveling together."

Hell of a coincidence, though, considering Ivan Anisimov had been found where someone hacked into the Pentagon—a task Dmitry could have done with ease.

"I checked that as well. Wanted to be sure before I involved you. Both tickets were purchased together. We're still looking into finding out the source of the buyer. It wasn't bought or paid for under either Anisimov or Ivanov's names."

Lucas considered Dmitry's burn alias, his fake persona. It was an identity even the Russian Government couldn't trace, and Lucas began to wonder why he would need such a thing. Something didn't feel right.

"I don't believe this to be the work of Dmitry. I've seen the man work. If he wanted to get in and out without being detected, he could have," Lucas said. "If he did infiltrate the system, he set the alarms off on purpose because he *wanted* to be found."

Chapter 9

Opening the external door to his kitchen, Lucas immediately sensed he wasn't alone. The air inside the room smelled different. He removed his weapon from his belt holster and held it out, away from his body, ready to fire if or when needed. He controlled his breathing, bringing it to a steady inhale and exhale so he could listen for other noises as he silently moved toward the door separating the kitchen from the rest of the house.

A tall figure, cloaked in shadow, approached the doorway. Lucas kept his gun at the ready, his index finger barely touching the trigger. His stare remained fixed on the man before him while his mind assessed the situation. Early morning daylight spilled through the window, the curtain drawn, and streaked across the face of his intruder as he stepped into the beam.

"Jesus Christ, Dmitry," he scolded. "I could have damn near shot you."

Dmitry leaned a heavy hip against the entryway into the kitchen, as if he no longer had the strength to keep standing. He let out a deep sigh, one that told Lucas he'd tried to think of other ways of dealing with his problem without having to involve him. "Sorry, Lucas, but I need your help."

"No shit." The Department of Defense had brought in the best cyber team to create an all new security system, the tech geeks working overnight so the firewall could go live that morning. They had yet to hear from the Pentagon in regards to what exactly had been stolen, but he knew it had to be big—like 9/11 big. Of course Dmitry needed his help.

He, along with the every law enforcement officer available, had been out all night trying to track Dmitry down, though his involvement was for a different purpose. He never thought of looking in his own home.

The man glanced about the room quickly before his gaze, showing vulnerability, turned back to Lucas. When he spoke, his voice came out childlike and uncertain. "You did say if Elena or I ever needed anything, we should come to you?"

He nodded, feeling like a bastard. He'd been in a similar situation and knew how lonely and scared he had been, hunted and all alone in a foreign city. Only difference was, he had Elena. Now, Dmitry had him. "Yes, I did. But I was expecting a knock on my door or a call first. You could have a least announced yourself with a light on or something."

Dmitry looked pained and relieved at the same time. "I didn't want anyone to know I was here. I'm in big trouble, Lucas."

"I know. They found Ivan."

Dmitry's already fair skin paled. He looked like he was about to drop any second. He ran a hand through his thick, dark hair and Lucas could see the fine mist collecting in his eyes. He pretended not to notice.

"He was my friend," Dmitry said. "I saw him murdered. It wasn't my idea. It was supposed to be a normal business meeting. I didn't come to Washington to hack the DoD."

He spoke imploringly, as if frightened Lucas would think he was the guilty party, or at least a willing participant.

Lucas held up his hands. "Relax, Dmitry. I believe you. That's not the problem. Getting my country to believe you is another matter. At the moment, they're a little trigger happy."

He noticed the way Dmitry held his arm tight against his chest, clearly not wanting to jar it, and listened as a gasp passed through his tightened lips. The look of pain etched on his ashen face was clear.

"You all right, man?"

Dmitry stepped into the light, and for the first time he saw the blood and torn shirt. He was surprised Dmitry was still on his feet. Whatever drove him had begun to run low, as he watched Dmitry try to stand straight. It was like watching a spinning top, wobbling side to side. It amazed him what the human body could withstand when pushed beyond the limit.

"Shit, Dmitry. Sit down. We'll have to clean you up or Elena's going to kill me."

Dmitry smiled as he sat, or rather collapsed, at the IKEA standard package kitchen table.

The reminder of Elena had been enough to give him superhuman strength just so he could make it home to her. Lucas remembered how he'd pushed himself all those months ago when he'd been so close to drowning, his water logged winter coat pulling him down into the dark, freezing water of the river Neva in St Petersburg. He'd felt like he was being stabbed repeatedly, but he'd wanted to ensure she was safe and had surfaced to find her, frantically calling to him. She was his light. A wonderful, caring woman with a heart of gold and looks to match.

"She will, don't you worry," Dmitry croaked. "She's always been a big old mama bear, that one."

Lucas got busy and moved about the kitchen, collecting his first aid kit and a bowl of warm water and a clean cloth. By the time he was done, Dmitry had his shirt off. Lucas squinted at the bloody wound.

Not too bad.

He began cleaning around the edges. Luckily, it was a through and through, otherwise he'd be getting out his little tweezers to dig into Dmitry's flesh and remove the bullet. In this case, Dmitry must have someone high up looking out for him today. No torn muscles or tendons, no veins or damaged ligature. He'll be sore for a few days but when he healed he'd have a nice scar to show the ladies, and told Dmitry so.

After a moment of silence, he asked, "Have you spoken with Elena yet?"

Dmitry shook his head so fast Lucas thought it might fly off. He knew the reason he felt reluctant.

Lucas understood, but he knew if he kept this from Elena he might as well kiss any relationship he might have with her goodbye. The angel of a woman could have a bitch of a temper if so inclined.

"I don't want to worry her," Dmitry admitted.

Lucas knew the last thing Dmitry wanted to do was to call Elena and tell her he fucked up big time. She would be on the first plane bound for Washington and he wouldn't want that. He would want to stand on his own two feet, as impossible as it sounded in his current predicament. As much as Dmitry wouldn't want his big sister coming to his rescue, the truth was he could use all the help he could get, including Elena's sway as an SVR agent. This was serious, and she would never forgive him if he left her out of this.

"I know, Dmitry, and I agree. But we both know Elena will not see it that way and she'll more than likely castrate the both of us. You know she'll give you hell if she finds out from someone else. She needs to know. You're in big trouble and she can help."

Dmitry's jaw clenched. He clearly didn't like the idea, but went along with it. Lucas picked up his phone from the newly renovated granite kitchen counter, and dialed the number from memory. He had slowly been renovating his house, hoping to make it a place a woman would love to visit. He'd thought of her while redoing the bedroom and master bath. It all came down to Elena, he knew that. Everything he'd done in the last eighteen months had been because of her. He'd done quite a bit of re-evaluating of his life since his time in Moscow, and he didn't want to give Elena any reason to say no to him.

She picked up within three rings. Her voice was full of enthusiasm as she greeted him in Russian. "*Privyet.*"

He ignored the slight flutter in his chest that always happened when he talked to her. "Elena."

He could hear the smile in her voice as she spoke, her tone friendly. "Lucas, I haven't heard from you in a while. It's a lovely surprise."

His body began to warm as he pictured her. She did things to him that no other woman ever had, and that was only with her voice. He didn't dare to imagine the things she could do to him if she was in the same room with him. Especially not with her brother nearby.

"Yes, it is." He cleared his throat. "Actually, the reason I'm calling is that there's someone here who wants to have a word with you."

Dmitry shook his head and raised his hands, refusing to take the phone from him. Lucas sent him a glare. Dmitry let out a deep breath before reluctantly taking the phone from him.

"Elena," he said.

Lucas thought he heard her asking if he was okay, and Dmitry gave her a condensed version, omitting certain key facts. Her voice rose with her panic before moving on to scolding him. He could hear her switching frantically between Russian and English, betraying her worry.

He raised an eyebrow. He could just make out some of what she was saying. For the past eighteen months, he had been taking a Russian language course, determined to learn to speak it even if it killed him. At the moment, he could keep up with a conversation as long as the words were spoken slowly.

Dmitry looked up at him, imploring him to help. Elena continued scolding him, not allowing him to get a word in. Lucas crossed the room to stand before Dmitry and reached out and took the phone. He shook his head at the younger man for allowing her to command the conversation, but then again, he figured even big shot criminals were apt to cringe under the sharp and admonishing tongues of their mothers or sisters.

"Don't worry, Elena, I have everything under control," he said calmly, interrupting her. He only hoped it was true. She stopped talking, and he heard her take a deep breath as if trying to calm herself.

"He's all I have left, Lucas. Please make him be careful," she said softly, her voice almost quivering.

She wasn't entirely correct. She still had him, but now wasn't the time or place to get into that. "I promise," he said before hanging up.

Then he looked at Dmitry. "Okay, you need to tell me everything from the start."

Chapter 10

Sitting across from his boss, a man of power and influence, Sean felt inadequate. Normally confident, he hated feeling like he couldn't compare. A smart man neither crossed nor failed the boss. Those who did ended in a bad way. He didn't plan on being one of them.

Dmitry Ivanov had disappeared, but he wasn't concerned. There was no place he could hide, not for long. He'd probably taken to the streets. Sean had ears to the ground. The Russian had no ties to America. He'd ensured that, monitoring the man's communiqués for months, Ivanov not once contacting anyone in the States. He was alone in a foreign land. It was only a matter of time until Sean got a whiff of him.

The boss looked up from the newspaper he had been reading and glared at him. Sean had been peddling drugs on a street corner when the boss had offered him a more elevated position with the resources of the government at his disposal—along with a back door into the Capitol, where he provided specific pharmaceuticals to money men whose decisions shaped the country.

The boss carefully folded up his newspaper and placed it on the fancy white tablecloth in the expensive restaurant. Sean tried not to feel out of place. Even after rubbing elbows with the elite he still felt uncomfortable in such elaborate surroundings.

"Well?" the boss asked, and Sean shifted nervously in his seat. He could always make him feel like a child again, giving him a sense that he'd disappointed him, somehow offending him personally. It annoyed him immensely.

"He got away," he said, still feeling the sting. "I wasn't expecting a double cross. It took me by surprise. I didn't think the bastard had the balls to pull anything."

He was sure the boss knew exactly what had gone down, and could bet within minutes of the Pentagon being alerted, he had also been informed.

"And where is Sundown now?"

He glanced around, ensuring they couldn't be overheard. He needn't bother. The boss frequented this location for its privacy and anonymity, the establishment renowned for confidentiality.

"I have no idea. Ivanov did something to the computer. When the alarm went off, the computer went on the fritz or something. The file downloaded and was sent away."

He was still pissed that the commie bastard had put one over on him. He wasn't an intelligent man by society's standards, had never gone to college and didn't have a fancy degree, but he had street smarts which always proved more useful in his line of business. He'd risen fast from the gutters, inspired by the men of the world who'd made something out of nothing. He planned to do just that, become an entrepreneur. Live his life in comfort and luxury.

"We must get Dmitry Ivanov back. Alive and in one piece," the boss said. Sean wondered if he also knew about his attempt to kill the Russian. He hoped not. It wasn't another failure, but the boss would hardly be happy about it. It hadn't been his finest hour and he'd since calmed down enough to realize how stupid a plan it had been. He needed Sundown just as much as the boss did.

"He must retrieve Sundown before someone else does," the boss continued. "The entire nation's security is tied up in that file. We're practically sitting ducks this very moment. A bad position, should our enemies discover that fact."

Sean nodded. He didn't care for the boss's political agenda. He was out for his own. He already had a couple of buyers in other countries who wanted Sundown, and the bidding had gone up to twenty million euros. He had no idea what that was in American dollars, but he was well aware that euros trumped dollars. With that kind of dough, he could retire to a nice non-extradition island. He didn't care if he could never return to the States again. It wasn't as if the country had ever done anything for him.

"Yeah, well, I'm looking into it. Ivanov and his partner Anisimov booked into a hotel near Dupont Circle. So far he hasn't shown up."

He would be stupid to do so. It hadn't taken the Department of Defense long to connect the dots, but the moment Ivanov's name was linked to Anisimov's, his fate was sealed. The entire company of American Federal Agencies had him on their watch list. He was fucked wherever he went. He just had to get to him first.

The boss linked his fingers together. "I want to know everything there is to know about this Dmitry Ivanov."

The man was practically a ghost. He had an apartment in the Moscow neighborhood of Belorusskaya-Radialnaya, had been living there for the past four and half years, yet he had no outstanding debts, no unaccountable funds or strange deposits. His record was clean.

At least it had been. He'd experienced a moment of concern when he'd learned Ivanov had one older sister, Elena—married name Nagregor—who worked for the Russian Government. That could be a problem. Or not. Though an agent, she was merely a liaison with no real power and due to the nature of her brother's crime, Russia would unlikely intercede on his behalf.

Still, he planned to monitor her movements. It never hurt to be cautious, especially now that he was so close to achieving his goals. He only hoped Dmitry loved his sister enough not to involve her.

He would hate to unnecessarily dispose of the woman. Although, perhaps she was the pressure point he'd been searching for.

Chapter 11

Elena barely felt the plane touch down at Dulles International Airport, her body tense with worry. She had spent the entire flight awake, her stomach twisting inside her until she felt sick. She couldn't believe this was happening.

Only a while ago, she and Lucas had been in trouble, and now it was her little brother. She had given a lot of thought into how she could help him. So far she had found nothing. She would have to wait and hear what the Americans said before she could really put a plan into motion.

After getting off the phone with Dmitry, she'd immediately booked a flight and was now more than ever determined to help him through his current predicament. She had awoken her boss, Director Vladimir Mishkin, who had not been happy about the early morning wake up call. She had told him firmly that she was taking some time off, and didn't elaborate as to why. Now she was in Washington, sleep deprived and jet lagged. She had dark circles under her grey eyes and her ponytail was mussed from leaning against the back of the seat. She was surly and hungry and desperately needed coffee.

First things first.

She hailed a yellow taxi-cab and gave the driver Lucas's home address. He had given her the address and the location of his spare key in case she ever visited Washington and he wasn't nearby to pick her up or let her in. This was the first time she would be using either.

The thought of him made her heart pound and her stomach flutter. He sent her body wild, craving things her dormant hormones hadn't thought of in years. She had been shocked at how she'd responded to him when they'd first met. She had been grieving for so long she'd tended to believe the male of species no longer existed, until she saw Lucas Gates. With his blond hair and blue eyes, he looked the quintessential California beach boy. No one could have thought him an excellent marksman, or saw him for the lethal fighter he was. He was also kind and considerate and had comforted her more than once during their adventure.

She'd not seen him in over a year and a half, but she would never forget his hard, well-toned body, or how he'd made her skin burn hot. It had reached the point where all she'd thought about was getting him alone and naked, with whipped cream and strawberries nearby. Seeing him again wouldn't be easy. He muddled her mind, all thoughts turning to mush when he was around.

She looked out the window at the early morning traffic passing her by on the way to his home in

Annandale. After eighteen months of denying and arguing with herself that there was nothing for her in America, she now found herself wishing she had come sooner. Washington was different from Moscow in many ways, yet she felt at home. Like she had always been meant to come over the seas and settle here. She shook her head at the fanciful thought, and bit into her bottom lip.

What would she do about Lucas? Not only had she been unable to come up with a sufficient plan for Dmitry, but she was also similarly stumped over the man whose image kept popping in her head. Lucas had been the foremost thought in her mind for the past eighteen months, dreaming about him, always thinking of him when she awoke. She loved him, and she'd known since that day at the airport when she'd watched him walk away. Her heart hadn't been ready, and she'd been quite content repressing those feelings, but now she felt free, lighter.

What if he no longer wanted her? The thought that had haunted her for the past month popped into her head and made her heart ache. She wasn't above begging for a second chance. She wanted Lucas and would fight for him if need be. She only wished she hadn't taken so long to decide.

She'd thought a lot about packing up her things and making a new life for herself in the States, had even gone as far as to get some boxes together. She'd get to box number three before she began hyperventilating and would not stop until all the boxes had been unpacked.

She was scared. She knew that. Nikolai, her

husband, had been brutally torn away from her, and truth be told, Lucas did sometimes remind her of him. They were both strong, independent men. They both had morals and a sense to do the right thing. To fight for justice and freedom.

During their short time together in Russia, she had found herself falling for him and wondered if that was the reason. Was she just replacing Nikolai with someone like him? She couldn't bear to think that way, or to use Lucas like that, so she had taken the space he had given her to try to understand her feelings. She had come to see that although they were both similar, she loved Lucas for who he was.

She would never get over losing Nikolai. They had so little time together, and while she would never stop loving him, there was room in her heart for Lucas too. She loved him—not in the same way as Nikolai, but equally as strong. How could she not? He was simply perfect in every way. He'd been there for her, understood her need to move past her grief before even contemplating a future with him, and had given her space. Too much space, in fact. She had started to feel unsure on top of her already fragile feelings. That, and because Lucas worked in a high risk job, had her emotions scattered all over the place.

No, this is definitely not going to be easy.

She spent the next twenty minutes alone with her muddled thoughts as an early morning radio show murmured in the background. Her feelings remained a jumble and she was no closer to sorting herself out. Her stomach turned as she tried to focus on the song playing through the cheap speakers in the cab.

After a series of twists and turns, the taxi stopped at the front of a single level square red brick house with white trimmings and a maroon door. The grass had been cut recently and the small garden bed had been weeded. An American flag stood proudly in the yard and gently fluttered in the breeze. A long waist height hedge lined the footpath and separated the street from the front lawn, neat and clipped. Certainly not something she would've associated with Lucas. She had expected a one bedroom bachelor pad apartment in the heart of the city, complete with smelly socks on the floor and week-old Chinese food in the refrigerator. Instead, she found a home that made her think of a stereotypical 1960s family sitcom.

But then, Lucas always did surprise her. He had more layers than an onion. She paid the driver and yanked her small suitcase down the paved path leading to the rear entrance where Lucas had told her the spare key was hidden. She hiked her purse higher on her shoulder and steeled herself for the emotional attack she knew lay just beyond the other side of the door.

Chapter 12

Dmitry stiffened as the external door to the kitchen opened. Lucas reached for his weapon, assessing for any potential danger. He caught a glimpse of light brown, almost blonde hair and the scent of gardenias filled his nostrils as recognition set in. He noticed Lucas tense where he sat, recognizing Elena's signature scent as she burst through the door, her gaze focusing on him. He grimaced at the stormy look on her face.

What the hell did she do, catch the redeye from Moscow to Washington? It'd been barely twenty-four hours since he'd spoken with her. He should've known she would come.

She stalked over to him, bypassing Lucas without a glance as the man's eyes feasted on her. Damn, did Lucas have it bad.

Ensuring the white bandage was hidden beneath his borrowed shirt, he prepared himself for his sister's anger.

"What's going on, Dmitry?" Elena snapped, spiraling into a lecture. He waited, knowing fear for his safety fueled her anger. When she was finished shouting at him, she continued, firing out questions like a machine gun. "Are you okay? How could this happen? You were supposed to be the smart one in the family." Her hands settled on her hips as she waited for his answer. Despite almost being a man of thirty, he'd always be her little brother and sometimes he resented that fact.

Dmitry set down the knife he'd been using to butter his toast and stood, using his size to intimidate her and ultimately to get her to back off. The attempt was unsuccessful. She appeared unconcerned and simply glared up at him.

"I told you hacking would lead to trouble, didn't I?"

There was nothing worse than letting someone down, particularly Elena. For so long, they'd only had each other to rely on. She had sacrificed a lot for him over the years after their parents had died. He hated knowing he was hurting her, even unintentionally.

He glanced over at Lucas, who stared at Elena like he'd never seen anything like her before.

Oh, spare me.

Here he was getting yelled at, and Lucas continued admiring Elena, who had yet to acknowledge his presence.

He drowned out Elena's lecture as he remembered the first time he'd met Lucas, when the man had come to his apartment, cold, tired and wearing a grey *Ushanka*—a traditional Russian hat with ear flaps—that Elena had bought him to disguise his American looks. He had immediately liked the man and offered his sister a little advice that she'd yet to take, which had been to pursue a relationship with Lucas.

He once again felt bad for the man, knowing Lucas had been waiting all this time for her and in a way he felt Elena had been waiting for him. He turned his attention back to her, while she continued lecturing about being caught up in an international event, citing hers and Lucas's incident as an example proving he should have learned from their mistakes.

In an effort to get her off his back, he said, "Look, Elena, it's Lucas."

It was a rather lame attempt, but it appeared to work. Like a small child distracted by a shiny bauble, Elena turned slowly and her gaze found Lucas.

Dmitry watched, amazed as her once angry red face softened, and he could have sworn he saw her expression melt into obvious affection.

Yuck! Shoot me if I ever look at a woman like that, he thought, as Elena's attention focused entirely on Lucas.

***

Lucas drank in the sight of her. She was more beautiful than he remembered, and her light hair had grown a few inches longer. He ached to run his fingers through it.

"Hello, Lucas," Elena said softly as her gaze found his, and a hint of a smile appeared on her luscious lips.

"Elena," he murmured.

God, he had missed her, and here she was—finally. If he stretched out his arm, he could touch her, feel her warm skin beneath his own. He didn't want to let her out of his sight, afraid she might disappear at any moment. He'd waited so long to get her to America and now that she was here, he would try his damnedest to make her stay. He wasn't above using every trick in the book.

He was bursting with impatience to find out how she felt about him and what the hell she planned to do about it. Other than that last day together at the airport, she'd never once hinted to her feelings and neither had he, unable to put himself out there in case she couldn't reciprocate. As much as it killed him, he could wait. He'd been waiting eighteen months now; a few more hours or days weren't going to make much difference. Damn, it felt like he'd been waiting forever. But she was worth it. That was the one thing that kept him going, knowing that she was out there and they could be together. Hopefully.

Her gaze drifted back to her brother, and she frowned. He stepped forward, drawing her attention once more, and took charge.

"I'm sure after that long flight you'll want to have a shower," he said. "I'll make you some coffee."

He took her by her arm and led her down the hall to the bathroom, watching as she tried to keep up with him. He controlled his urge to grin at the baffled expression on her face.

"Are you in the mood for breakfast?" he asked

before turning on the faucet in the shower. The water sprayed into the glass capsule, against the large black and white checkered tiles. She stared at him blankly, still processing everything. He stepped away from her before he had the insane idea to remove all her clothes. It wouldn't be a hard task, but by God he would be hard by the end of it. The desire already coursed through his veins, his blood heating, all thoughts heading south.

She placed her hand on his arm and he tensed, afraid he'd act on some of the fantasies bouncing around his head. His knees almost buckled when his gaze met hers, the lost look in those cool grey depths squeezing at his heart.

"Thank you, Lucas, for everything. I know you're risking your career by helping Dmitry. I appreciate all you've done to keep him safe."

He ran his hand over her soft cheek. Her lips parted. "I like Dmitry. I believe in his innocence, but I'm not doing this for him…at least not only him."

Her lips parted in an *O* as she blinked owlishly at him, obviously unsure how to reply to his comment. That was fine. They had time. But if she thought she was leaving before they had a conversation, she had another thing coming.

Kissing her forehead, he took a deep breath, inhaling the sweet scent of gardenias, and quickly moved out of the bathroom, closing the door firmly behind him without waiting for a reply. Let her think on that while he got himself under control. He'd been close to throwing her down on the cold tiled floor and imbedding himself deep inside her, losing himself to nothing but the feel of her body closing around his own.

He took off for the kitchen, trying to clear his mind of the thought of her in his shower, naked and wet, soap suds sliding sensuously down her soft skin. He thumped the frying pan down on the stove top and greased it, then turned to find Dmitry grinning at him.

He felt like smacking the bastard. Dmitry knew exactly what effect his sister had on him.

Just you wait, Dmitry. One day it will be you, mesmerized by some woman.

"Don't you dare say another word," he warned, "or I won't run interference for you ever again."

Dmitry's grin slipped away. Ten minutes later, Elena graced them with her presence, wearing black trousers with matching black leather boots and a cream blouse that highlighted her curves. Her light colored hair hung past her shoulders in gentle waves. She flopped down heavily in a chair at the table as he placed the freshly cooked plate of eggs and bacon, along with a mug of coffee, in front of her. Smiling at him gratefully, her stomach growled and she dug in.

"How the hell did you and Ivan get entangled in this?" she asked around a mouthful of food.

"You know Ivan and I started a business not long ago. Freelance stuff. Computer programming. Specialized software building, that sort of thing. Word spread."

Elena nodded. "So how is it he's dead and you're on the run?"

Lucas grimaced, but Dmitry didn't seem to take

offense. He continued with his story. "Ivan got us a contract with an American client. Not government," he added, when he saw she was about to interrupt. "Or at least I didn't think that was the case. I'm not so sure now. It was all expenses paid—flight, hotel, plus hours on top. All we had to do was come here, view their business, and create a system to help them run more efficiently. I did have some concerns about why they hired us, and there were a few red flags, but the money was so good we said yes. We're new on the scene, but Ivan said this was our big chance, and eventually I didn't ask any more questions."

Elena took another bite before washing it down with a sip of coffee. "What happened when you got here?"

"They wanted to get started right away, so we arranged for a rental and drove to the warehouse. I knew something was wrong when the man handed me a government IP address. I declined the job. Ivan was shot and then the gun was pointed at me. I did what I could under the circumstances to stay alive."

Elena put her hand over his. "I'm sorry about Ivan, Dmitry. And I'm sorry for being so hard on you. I know you did the best you could. I was just scared thinking I might've lost you."

Dmitry squeezed her hand in return. Elena's eyes glistened. He'd seen Elena in tears before, just after SVR had shot at them and chased them all over Moscow. It had been the first time he'd held her. His arms itched to pull her close and comfort her as he'd done that day, but instead he stayed away. If he touched her now, he would never let her go, and Dmitry needed their help.

"He was a good friend," Dmitry said, his voice thick with emotion.

Elena held his hand tightly with both of hers, and sniffled. "I'm so sorry."

Lucas took a step closer to the siblings. "You mentioned something about Sundown. What's that?" he asked, interrupting the emotional tide.

"The man who shot Ivan introduced himself as Stephen Hosking, but I doubt that's his real name. He asked me to access a file named Sundown. I have no idea what it is." He let out a deep sigh and ran his uninjured hand through his dark hair. "I knew I couldn't let him get his hands on it, so I made sure to set off the alarm at DoD which would trigger the file to disperse out to hundreds of different locations around the world. It was a program of my design created to stop hackers from getting classified information. I never planned on using it myself."

Lucas slapped his thigh. "I knew it. I knew when the alarm went off it was intentional. You're too good a hacker not to bypass the alarm."

Elena glared at him. She obviously didn't appreciate his enthusiasm over her brother's abilities. "Can't you just access your program and recall Sundown?"

"I would, but when I downloaded Sundown the file was tagged. The moment I try, I can guarantee government vehicles will pull up in the driveway."

Lucas cursed.

"I'll work on a program to jam the tag reporting

back to DoD. Until then…" They had to wait.

"Well, the only way to appease the posse will be to hand over Sundown." Lucas thought aloud, referring to the government. "Since retrieving the file now is not an option, I think we're all in agreement. You'll remain here out of sight."

Elena nodded and stepped around the table to hug her brother.

"We'll go to Langley and see just how much trouble our boy is in," Lucas decided, his gaze on Elena, "then swing by the morgue so you can make arrangements for Ivan."

She sent him a look of appreciation. One he felt all the way down to his toes. His heart clenched painfully in his chest. "Meanwhile, Dmitry," Elena said, "I want you to find out everything you can about the man who hired you. Do whatever you have to. I want a name."

Elena wasn't the only one who wanted to have a chat with the man. Lucas had a few choice words also. Dmitry looked about the kitchen at the polished bench tops and stainless steel sink with matching appliances towards the timber hutch in the corner. "And how exactly am I supposed to do this? On my iPhone? It could be done, but it'll be a real pain in the ass."

Lucas scowled. "I have a computer you can use."

Elena and Dmitry followed him into a small nook off the dining area. A large old-fashioned box monitor sat on a desk beside his rather antiquated printer and fax. Dmitry's eyebrow rose when he took in the sight of the monitor.

"Do you even have Internet?" he asked,

switching on the computer and waiting while it started up. The machine wheezed as the fan worked hard to remove the thick coat of dust that had settled within the computer's internal components. He groaned when he saw the screen display the Windows 2000 logo. He turned and faced Lucas. "You know that operating system is over a decade old, right?"

Elena fought a smile. "You're such a technology snob."

"It works. That's all that matters," Lucas retorted. "Beggars can't be choosers."

He'd never been good at keeping up with the latest technology, and refused to upgrade unless his previous equipment had died or when he bought a new system that had become outdated. Since he rarely used his home computer, often opting to use the one he had at work, he never felt the need to purchase anything new.

Elena shook her head and patted Dmitry's back in sympathy.

"When you get me out of this mess, I'm fixing you up. Get you out of the dark ages." Dmitry sat down and clicked on the Internet Explorer icon, adding, "I hope it's not dial-up."

The home page came up almost immediately and Dmitry let out a relieved breath before he started tapping away at the keyboard, his concentration fierce.

Lucas doubted Dmitry even realized he and Elena were still in the room. He glanced over at her and caught her gaze, then took her hand—just because he needed to touch her—and pulled her close, savoring the feel of her against him before leading her out of the room, leaving Dmitry to his work.

Chapter 13

James Fitzgibbon stood as Lucas entered his office, escorting a woman. The younger man had his hand placed possessively on her back. He moved from behind his desk to greet them both.

This must be Elena Ivanova, he thought as he subtly gave her a once over.

She was beautiful, with sharp Slavic cheekbones and cool grey eyes. He could easily understand why Lucas had become so enamored of her. She stood several inches shorter than Lucas, her body generously curvy. She smiled as he approached, transforming her face from beautiful to breathtaking. Lucas was one lucky bastard.

"I am James Fitzgibbon, Agent Ivanova. I've been expecting you."

Elena glanced at Lucas, surprise evident on her face. Lucas gave her a reassuring smile.

"Yes, I suppose you have," she said, turning away from Lucas. "It's great to finally meet you, SAC Fitzgibbon." She held out her hand for him to shake, and he took her delicate fingers in his giant palm and marveled at the softness of her skin. Even after decades of marriage, he was still amazed at how delicate a woman was compared to a man—something he tended to forget when his lovely, sweet wife screamed at him for one of his many infractions. Elena had a very strong, firm handshake. He liked that.

"Please call me Jim, Elena. All my friends do, and I consider you a friend. After all, you did get my boy Lucas out of trouble. Now I'd like to repay the favor."

Elena had stuck by Lucas the entire time he'd been in Moscow. She had even gone up against and defied her own agency to protect him, resulting in her being shot at and chased by her own people. He felt indebted to her for that. He also knew from Lucas that she was very good at her job, something else he admired. He loved a patriot who was dedicated to his or her work.

Agent Elena Ivanova was both. They'd get along just fine—as long as she didn't break Lucas's heart. Lucas was the closest thing to a son that he and his wife Maggie ever had, and both of them were extremely protective of their boy. So far, he'd never approved of any of the women Lucas had bothered to introduce. But all that changed the moment Elena Ivanova walked in. She was just the woman to keep Lucas in line and relatively under control—if such a thing was possible. She could love him like he deserved to be loved. Jim only hoped it worked out for the both of them.

Elena blushed. "It was nothing. I was glad to help. Once I got over cursing him for involving me, of course," she added. "But it all worked out in the end and I don't regret a moment of it—except maybe jumping out my second floor apartment window and the visit to the not-so-friendly neighborhood mob."

The intimate glance she sent toward Lucas spoke of unfulfilled promises and heart-aching tenderness. He looked away, uncomfortable being privy to what should've been a private moment. If he'd had any doubts as to Elena's feelings, they'd all been put to rest. She would have never made a good poker player; her thoughts were as clear as day to him.

"Lucas has never been one to toe the line," he said.

Despite this, he couldn't fault the results, and never once regretted the decision to make him a part of the team. Although he had caused more than one grey hair on his head, Lucas was a man with principals and nothing could sway him. It was what made him such a great agent and a man Jim was proud to know.

"Yes. I soon learned that," Elena said, wry humor in her voice. "It was an interesting learning curve."

"I can imagine."

"It all worked out in the end." She surreptitiously gave Lucas a glance, then looked back at Jim. She took an unsteady breath as she moved the conversation towards the reason she was here. "I understand you have quite the case on my brother. If you don't mind, I would like to review the list of charges you have against him."

Her manner was profession, her tone cool but he

sensed the emotions beneath the surface. He didn't envy her situation one bit. "Of course. This is current as of nine this morning. The DoD is continually adding to it. They're after blood, I'm afraid."

He pulled out two sheets of paper from the stack on his desk and handed them to her, watching as her eyes widened while she surveyed the charges. He didn't blame her. Dmitry Ivanov was a wanted man. His hacking into the DoD had put him on every terrorist watch list in the United States, and he'd probably be added to an international list as well.

Should he be put on trial, the likelihood of him ever being released was small and if by some miracle that day ever came, there would be certain stipulations—such as he'd never be able to touch another computer for the rest of his life. For a man who lived and breathed technology, it would be a fate worse than death.

He eyed Lucas, who also read the list of charges over Elena's shoulder. "You wouldn't be stupid enough to harbor a criminal, now would you, Lucas?"

Both glanced up from the paper to meet his stare. He noted the blank expressions that showed no emotion; they could have been talking about the weather for all the feeling they revealed.

"Of course not," Lucas said without hesitation.

Despite this, Jim knew he would find Dmitry Ivanov stashed away at Lucas's residence, if he chose to search. He wouldn't. Lucas was fiercely loyal to his friends and those he considered family, which meant he would do just about anything for

Elena.

Someone knocked at the door, and a tall bulky man dressed in a smart blue suit entered. Jim made the introductions.

"Secretary Mann," he said, greeting the Secretary of Defense. "Thank you for coming. This is Agent Lucas Gates of my team, and Agent Elena Ivanova. She's with Russian Intelligence."

Mann nodded in greeting, a barely perceived movement. Jim had never much liked the secretary, who he found to be arrogant and self-entitled. Two things he hated in a person.

"Tell us about Sundown," he suggested politely, despite it not being a request. If they were to help Dmitry—and there was no question they would—they needed to understand the magnitude of what they were dealing with and the possible backlash. He never even bothered to ask if the Russian was guilty. He trusted Lucas's judgment as much as his own, and if Lucas was positive of the man's innocence that was enough for him.

Plus, he owed Elena for saving Lucas's life.

Mann's dark gaze looked about the room as if confirming the four of them were alone.

"I can guarantee we all have the suitable clearance, Secretary," Jim assured him. "What you are about to say will not leave this room."

He didn't seem appeased, but continued regardless. "Sundown is the DoD's new sixty billion dollar security protocol and implementation for the country. It includes everything from the locations of our nuclear weapons to the men qualified to release them. It also contains the

President's new Armageddon strategies, and the data back-up and storage locations."

"Are you telling us that the entire country's security is detailed in one complete file, downloadable from the DoD's mainframe?" he asked, incredulous. "Whose brilliant idea was that?"

Mann shifted awkwardly, and Jim realized why Secretary Fuck-up was ready to hang Ivanov out to dry by naming him this year's top terrorist. He was looking for a scapegoat.

"It was supposed to be secure. We hadn't expected anyone to bypass the Pentagon's firewalls," Mann admitted somewhat contritely.

Got to love the bureaucrats. They were idiots, as far as he was concerned. It didn't matter what level they were on. None of them had enough brain power to find their way out of a building with a map in their hands, and *these* were the people making the decisions for the country.

"Security is an illusion, Secretary Mann," Elena said. "Surely, you know this. Just because you have four walls and a ceiling does not mean you don't need locks."

Mann fixed his glare on her. "You realize the international crisis we have on our hands, young lady?" he snapped, his tone condescending.

She appeared to grit her teeth, seeming angered by the chauvinistic put-down, and probably also for the assumption she might not know how to do her job. Mann was wrong on all accounts. She was extremely qualified, and had been trained for many situations the secretary probably hadn't. When she answered, her words were carefully measured, her voice calm and devoid of any seething anger she obviously felt, if her face was any indication.

"You need to understand, Secretary Mann that I am not here on behalf on my country but as Dmitry Ivanov's sister."

Mann grunted. "You have your work cut out for you, then."

Elena's eyes darkened.

If looks could kill, we'd have a dead man.

"You have no unequivocal proof that my brother is guilty," Elena retorted, "only circumstantial evidence."

She had a backbone of pure steel, and he commended her for it. She was certainly an asset to her agency, and despite the fact that her brother's life was on the line, she kept her cool through the entire proceeding. If Jim had been in her place, he would've decked the man by now, and it was clear by Lucas's expression that he felt the same.

"I have more than enough for a conviction, I assure you," Mann replied. "The fact that your brother is not standing here today speaks volumes. Dmitry Ivanov is a known hacker, his skills legendary. Do you wish to continue to argue your brother's innocence to me? We both know he's guilty, and when he's found, he'll be punished to the full extent of the law."

Panic crept into Elena's eyes. Jim's gaze fell on her fingers as they twisted around the third finger on her left hand in an anxious gesture. It was almost as if she were winding a phantom ring and he realized that's exactly what she was doing. Beside her, Lucas stilled, her movements catching his attention and his sharp mind most likely processing she no longer wore her wedding band, her pale finger devoid of a tan line. It had been some time since she'd removed the last visible link to her husband.

Lucas shot the secretary a death look at impugning Dmitry's nature. Jim was fully aware how much Lucas admired and trusted the man. Any slight against Dmitry would also be against Lucas.

"You don't know my brother," Elena said. "He is a patriot. He would never willingly put anyone's life in danger."

Lucas placed his hand on Elena's back, and her stiff body softened as she leaned into his touch.

"I understand you want to protect your brother. Unfortunately, that time has passed. If he turns himself in now, the U.S. Attorney will take that into consideration."

"I will not send my brother to be unfairly accused."

"You have twenty-four hours to recover Sundown. If you fail, or if we find him first, your brother will be arrested on treason and attempted terrorism," Mann declared. "And you may be charged as an accessory."

Lucas stiffened.

"And what will you be charged with? Unwittingly putting the security of the nation in jeopardy?" she snapped.

The secretary's face turned red. "Now, see here Ms. Ivanova—"

"You address me as *Agent* Ivanova, Secretary Mann. Be sure to remember that. And I will not allow you to railroad my brother because of your foolish mistake."

"Although I appreciate your position, the truth is that your brother hacked the Department of Defense. That sort of thing isn't punishable by a mere slap on the hand. It'll be best if he gives himself up. The charges will be more lenient. I suggest you try to persuade him." Mann stalked out, slamming the door behind him.

Lucas stepped toward the window overlooking the parking lot, and stared out. Elena slumped into the visitor's chair and crossed her legs as Jim perched himself on the edge of his desk.

"He's screwed, isn't he?" Elena asked, sounding dejected. He could see she was fighting tears. "Even though he acted under duress. There's no way he can redeem himself."

"So he *is* guilty."

Elena gave him a look. "I never said he wasn't."

"Yes. I noticed that," he replied wryly. She was a very smart woman. Lucas would need to watch out. She was sure to keep him on his toes.

"When Dmitry called me in Moscow, he told me what happened and how Ivan was murdered. He knew they planned to kill him, too, once he retrieved the file, so he ran."

"Understandable. I take it you have him working on it now? If there's anyone who can get him out of this, it's Dmitry himself."

"We have him looking into the man who hired him, under false pretenses I might add."

He nodded. "Good. If you can find the man responsible, you can make your own case to take to the U.S. Attorney. I will be happy to provide support to your brother and back his character. Of course, I can't guarantee he will not be charged."

"Thank you for believing in him. You don't even know my brother."

"But I know you, and if he's anything like you, Dmitry Ivanov must be very special."

Elena appeared to relax. "Thank you," she said, rising from her seat. She surprised him by wrapping her arms around his ever-expanding form, and kissing him on the cheek. "Please don't do anything that could cost you your career," she added.

"My dear, if I can't help innocent, patriotic people, then what good is my career? I will not let a good man be persecuted."

She blinked back her tears, and gave him a grateful smile as she stepped back toward her chair.

"What about Sundown?" he asked. "Is it out in the open?"

"Yes and no. Dmitry is the only person in the country who can retrieve Sundown from its locations."

"Locations…as in more than one?"

Turning to face them, Lucas leaned against the wall. "Hundreds, actually."

He frowned. He didn't understand computers, let alone the skill and knowledge it took to bypass several security features he'd been told were impenetrable. He wouldn't even know where to start.

"My brother used one of his own programs, so that when the system was hacked, the information would be sent out to anonymous servers," she explained.

Lucas stepped forward. "Dmitry is good at what he does. He won't let anyone else get Sundown as long as he's alive. It's safe where it is—for now."

Elena chewed on her lower lip, drawing attention to her lush mouth. Even he, a happily married man, had a hard time ignoring her desirability. He could only imagine the torture Lucas experienced.

"Relax, Elena. We're not going to let anything happen to Dmitry," Lucas reassured her.

"I know, but I can't help but worry. At least until he's out of the woods. So much could happen before then."

"Such the pessimist."

"A realist. Where do we go from here?"

"We check in with Dmitry, see how it's going."

Elena snorted. "You can do that. My brother gets extremely annoyed when I interrupt him when he's in the zone."

Lucas's eyebrow rose. "I can't imagine Dmitry pissed."

"Oh, trust me, he can be cold and indifferent. But by all means call him and see for yourself. Speaking of, I need to check my messages. I'll just be a moment."

Lucas frowned and followed her to the door, watching as she walked down the hall. Jim chuckled from his desk, and Lucas scowled at him.

"What are you cackling about?" he demanded.

"You, my boy. Can't half tell what you're thinking and feeling. Got hit hard, didn't you? Well, about fucking time, and that little bombshell out there is just the woman to keep you in check."

"I hate that you know me so well."

"Give her time, Lucas. I don't think she quite knows what she wants at the moment. Her brother is in trouble. A friend has died. Any more on her plate, and she could collapse under the strain."

"I know." Lucas let out a deep breath as he ran stiff fingers through his blond hair. "I just need to know where we stand."

***

Elena cringed when she heard her boss's voice. He didn't sound happy—not that Vladimir ever did, but this time it seemed worse. She had an idea what had made the man so upset. She called him back straight away, deciding against prolonging the lecture. Best to get it over with so she could focus on Dmitry and getting him out of his current predicament. Then there was Lucas, something else she couldn't hold off any longer. She needed to hash out their relationship—if they had one. She needed to know once and for all if he still wanted her or if she'd lost her chance. She feared that the most. She had no one but herself to blame if Lucas had finally given up waiting for her and moved on. She felt tears burn in her eyes at the thought, and swallowed the lump in her throat.

She desperately needed to know the answer to her many questions. The not knowing only made things worse.

"Tell me you are not in Washington sticking your nose in their business," Vladimir Mishkin said instantly once the call connected.

"You've heard?" she asked, surprised. Her boss wasn't usually interested in foreign affairs. If it wasn't happening in Russia, he didn't hear about it.

"That your brother is wanted by American authorities for hacking into a secure government site?" he retorted. "Yes, I know, and I think you should leave this to your American friend to handle and get yourself back here on the next plane."

"You know I can't do that. I won't leave my brother to his fate."

She knew he'd be sent to Guantánamo Bay as a terrorist if caught, and she might never see him again. She would break any law to keep that from happening.

"You know I don't condone this kind of lone ranger behavior," Vladimir said. He always followed the rules, and at one time, so had she. Things changed when she met Lucas. "I gave you leeway last time due to unforeseeable circumstances," he continued, "but if you're not on a plane within twenty-four hours—"

"I understand, sir. If you don't see me in forty-eight hours, you won't see me at all."

She hung up and turned off the phone. She didn't want Director Mishkin calling her back, especially if she was unprepared to give him answers. She had dismissed his warning. It would take as long as it took, and she wouldn't leave Washington without her brother.

Chapter 14

Elena climbed into Lucas's government issued car, on edge and frightened. Her brother was being hounded by the American government, as well as the man who'd tried to kill him. She still had no idea how she could help him, and felt useless.

Then, there was Lucas. Her heart beat quicker in his presence. She wasn't even sure how to broach the subject of their relationship. Regardless, now wasn't the time.

They were on the way to the morgue on Massachusetts Avenue where Ivan's body was being held. Her nerves were already frayed, revved up for a fight. The arrogant secretary could do with being taken down a peg or two. She had a desire to ram Sundown into the man's throat until he choked. He was the one at fault for allowing the country's entire security protocol to be uploaded into cyberspace. Surely, he knew how vulnerable it could be despite being heavily guarded, and now because someone else wanted the bloody thing, he placed the blame squarely on Dmitry's relatively innocent shoulders. She would not let her baby brother take the fall, even if she had to declare war on the United States to achieve it.

She didn't even allow herself to think of Director Mishkin's ultimatum. She closed her eyes and wished for silence. There were so many threads in her mind, and the more she thought on them, the more tangled they became.

"Are you okay?"

Her head jerked toward Lucas. He'd been so quiet since they'd left Langley she'd almost forgotten he was there. *Almost* because no matter how distracted she was, in the back of her mind she was always aware of his proximity to her.

"No," she replied. "What part of this would make me okay?"

Instantly contrite, she apologized for her brusque reply. Lucas had been so wonderful to her, and certainly didn't deserve her snippy attitude. He was the one man who'd always stood beside her in a battle. She blinked at the tears gathering in her eyes. It seemed crying was all she'd been able to do since arriving in the States. It was humiliating. She hated being seen as weak and emotional, but she couldn't seem to stop herself. She wrapped her arms tightly around her body as if that was the very bind that kept her from shattering into a million pieces.

"You're not alone in this. I'm right here with you and I'm not going to let anything happen to Dmitry. I promise."

Her heart skipped a beat and her stomach did a flip. He promised; those two words meant everything to her. From a man whose word was the very embodiment of his being, it was about as secure as she could get.

Despite the niggling doubts she had about them. She closed her mind from those dark thoughts.

"Thank you, Lucas. That means a lot to me, and to Dmitry," she added, not wanting him to read too much into her words. The last thing she wanted was to make a fool of herself if he didn't want the same thing she did.

Her fingers moved to twist the ring on her finger, as she always did when she was anxious, only to find it naked. She hadn't worn her wedding band since Lucas had walked into her quiet life and disrupted it. From the moment she'd met Lucas, she had begun to feel as if she no longer belonged to Nikolai and didn't feel right wearing the ring he'd given her when her heart yearned for another. Most days, she didn't even notice it was gone but during moments of high stress she instinctively reached for the one thing that helped soothe her. She missed the loss acutely—a familiar thing she could cling to while everything around her fell apart.

Desperate not to show her discomfort, she twined her fingers together to keep them occupied and dropped her hands to her lap, hoping Lucas hadn't noticed her near panic attack.

"Dmitry's a good guy," he said. "He doesn't deserve any of the shit that's happened to him since he arrived, that's for goddamn sure."

"You're a good man, Lucas, you really are," she said, her voice quivering. She let out a deep sigh.

"Elena—"

She held up a hand, stopping him. "Don't. I just

want to get this over with and then you can take me to my hotel."

Lucas took his gaze off the road and gave her a long considering look for as long as he dared before returning his focus to the street.

"Hotel?" He shook his head. "No, Elena. You're staying with me. I've got plenty of room."

She chewed nervously on her bottom lip. "I don't want to impose. I wasn't sure—" She broke off, not wanting to ask the question. She knew she wouldn't be able to take the answer—either of the answers.

"What, that I might have changed my mind about us?"

A frustrated breath escaped, her mind muddled with too many thoughts. She could barely keep up with one thing let alone another, and wished she hadn't opened her mouth.

"Can we not talk about this just now?" she asked, her voice almost pleading. She was a coward. For all her talk about hashing things out, she was too afraid of walking away with nothing. What would she do without him? The pain inside her expanded and she almost gasped aloud. She'd never given that much thought to all her worrying over it, and now that the stark reality slapped her in the face she found herself terrified. She didn't think she could survive losing Lucas—especially not to her own stupidity. A tear escaped her eye and she quickly dashed it away.

Lucas pulled into the parking structure of the Metropolitan Morgue. He stopped at a large boom gate and showed his credentials to the guard on duty. When the barrier lifted, he drove through and parked the car further on down.

"We *will* talk about this," he said, following a brief silence between them.

She nodded as she gathered up her purse and followed him into the building. They found the bank of elevators and Lucas pressed the down button. She noticed the glass panel directory where it stood mounted to the wall above the elevator call button. The Metropolitan Morgue was in the sub-basement.

"So what did Mishkin want?" he asked. "You didn't look too happy when you got off the phone with him."

"How did you know it was Director Mishkin?"

"The tone of voice and the scowl on your face," he said. "I figured there was only one hobbit in all of Russia who could make you that mad."

Smiling, she smothered a giggle. Vladimir Mishkin was roughly her height, and they stood eye to eye, which meant Lucas towered over the little man. She'd always thought he looked a lot like a Russian Hercule Poirot. Mishkin and Lucas had never liked each other, ever since their first meeting in the conference room at SVR Headquarters. She remembered him telling her not long after they met that he only spoke two languages, English and body language, the latter having come in handy more than once.

"Oh, you know Mishkin. He doesn't approve of me being here and getting caught up in an American investigation." She waved her hand in dismissal, downplaying it as they entered the elevator. The lift doors closed, and they headed for the morgue.

***

Lucas watched her face closely, reading her. For a woman who hadn't gotten much sleep the previous night, clearly distressed over her brother, she looked really good. She had swiped her lashes with mascara, making her grey eyes seem larger, bringing more attention to her already beautiful face. She had also added some gloss to her naturally pink lips that made him want to taste them.

He sensed the tension beneath her words. There was something she wasn't telling him and he hated that she wouldn't confide in him. If only she'd let him in. "It's more than that, isn't it?"

She waved off his concerns, which annoyed him. "Nothing to be worried about, I assure you."

She gave him a smile that he didn't buy. He knew her too well to believe that. But he also knew if she wasn't willing to tell him, he wouldn't get an answer. Not without torture, at least. A few techniques came to mind, some he was dying to try out on her. He shook his head to clear it, then opened the outer door to the morgue and waited until an attendant arrived to escort them to the observation room.

"Dmitry's going to be fine, Elena. You know that, right?" He needed to know that she believed and trusted in him to help her.

"Yes, Lucas, I do. Between you and SAC Fitzgibbon, my brother is quite safe or at least will be by morning. Thank you. I don't think I got a chance to say so before, but I really am very appreciative of what you've done despite my complaints."

She could complain all she wanted, so long as she was near. He glanced down at her finger, noting the absence of her wedding ring. Did he dare to hope? He wouldn't push, not while she was so fragile, but soon they would hash this out. With any luck they'd be on the same page.

A tall thin man sporting a white lab coat and identification badge joined them. A faint scent of formaldehyde clung to the man's pores that no amount of scrubbing and washing would remove. His eyes were a warm blue and his hair a real ginger that seemed to stand straight up in the air without the use of gel.

"Agent Gates?" he asked him. Lucas nodded and introduced Elena before explaining that they were here to see Ivan Anisimov.

"Now, you're sure you want to see him like this? The decedent has already been identified. He's not a very pretty sight."

"That's all right," Elena said. "Believe me, I've seen worse."

"Okay, then. You've been warned. Follow me."

Chapter 15

Elena followed the attendant into the chilly viewing room. Directly ahead were the stainless steel body drawers, and she recalled how she'd always thought they looked like over-sized filing cabinets. It was probably true in a way. Bodies were stored there until either loved ones or the state had them removed for burial.

The attendant moved over to drawer number sixty-one and opened the small door, pulling out the attached platform with Ivan's body lying on top.

"I'll give you a minute. I'll be right over there," the attendant informed her, and she nodded as he moved away to the other side of the room to a work desk, where he promptly sat down and began sorting out some documents.

She looked down at the remains of the man she'd known for years. She could hardly believe it was the same person. Ivan had never let anything get him down. When he had failed at something—and he had often—he'd just gone out and started something new. He never had a whole lot of luck but it had seemed things were working out for him this time around with this new business venture of his with Dmitry. Tears stung her eyes and she fought to keep them at bay.

She remembered Ivan as a little boy, when he and Dmitry had done everything together including playing tricks on her, reading her diary and then blackmailing her with the contents. It wasn't until Ivan developed a crush on her at sixteen that the teasing stopped. From that moment, Ivan started following her around like a puppy dog, much to Dmitry's embarrassment. A boy of fourteen really couldn't understand his friend's fascination with his sister.

The even scarier thing for her was that this could have been Dmitry lying lifeless on the cold steel platform. A warm tear spilled over onto her cheek and she wiped it away carelessly. She would find the bastard who'd done this to Ivan. He would not get away with taking a good man's life. Maybe this was acceptable in America, but she had her own laws to obey and allowing a murderer to go free just wasn't one of them.

Lucas remained silently behind her, a steady rock in a raging river. She sensed his inner strength and his body heat seeped into her, warming her chilled one.

"There's a Russian Proverb. You don't get good apples from a bad tree," she said softly, her voice not quite steady. "But Ivan tried so hard to rid himself of his parents' stigma. They weren't very good people, constantly on the wrong side of the law, backing communist regimes. They weren't well favored and died when Ivan was quite young.

"He always made me smile. Even when I was infuriated with him, I'd end up laughing because of his antics. I loved him like a brother." She turned toward the attendant. "Are there forms I have to fill out to have him shipped back to Russia?"

The attendant looked up from his desk and nodded. "Yes. You will be the one making all the arrangements?"

She nodded. "I'm the only one in the country with ties to Ivan. I'll be happy to pay the fees for him to go home."

She placed a hand on Ivan's cold one. He hadn't deserved any of this.

"Okay, let me get them ready and we can have him shipped by the end of the week."

The attendant left the room in search of the forms. Lucas stepped forward and placed his hands on her shoulders, lending her silent support. She leaned her back against his chest, amazed at how natural it felt, then closed her eyes and allowed herself to experience his nearness. She breathed in his subtle scent, a mixture of soap and manliness. Her body was never her own when he was near. She'd never felt like this before. Not even with Nikolai.

"I'm so sorry, Elena," he said into her hair. His hands moved from her shoulders and wrapped around her small frame, placing his chin on her shoulder. "You know you can always cry around me. I don't care. In fact, I kind of like it."

His breath tickled her neck and a shiver shot down her spine. She struggled to keep her breathing even. "Easy for you to say. You're not the one making a fool of yourself."

Lucas smiled. "I don't know about that. I'd say being halfway frozen and naked on a boat would constitute as an embarrassing moment. I was hardly at my full glory."

Elena giggled as she remembered the time he spoke of. They had been fighting for their lives aboard Alexei's boat on the choppy river when Lucas had gone overboard. With the chilly November climate, he almost froze and caught hypothermia, and to save his life she had stripped him down to his underpants.

"You were wearing boxers."

"Still, it wasn't my finest hour."

She turned in his arms and burrowed her head into his chest as the first waves of sobs hit her. She gave into them and wrapped her arms around him, holding onto him as tightly as she could. So much was changing; so much had already changed and she was still trying to catch up.

She felt like she was drowning in the tidal wave slowly wreaking havoc on her life. It was hard seeing someone she cared about dead, especially when she didn't have many friends left in the world. Someone she'd known most of her life who was now nothing more than skin and bone, slowly deteriorating into something unrecognizable. No light. Nothing that made them who they'd been. Everyone seemed to be dying around her. First Nikolai, and now Ivan. Then there was Alexei's deception. It felt like a plague even though she knew that neither death had been her fault.

Lucas pulled her in tighter to him as he had done once back in Moscow. It was the only time she had felt completely safe. It had been the first time in a while that she had felt like everything was going to be all right and now he was doing it again. She was stunned at how he could comfort her so much by doing so little. She had missed the feeling, amazed that she could miss something she had never thought about before but she did—a lot. She could feel contentment rising within her.

"This is not how I wanted you to see America," Lucas said, breaking into the silence that had stretched between them as she'd struggled with her feelings. She hadn't minded it. She and Lucas had come to a point where any quiet times were comfortable between them and neither of them felt the need to fill the empty space.

Of course he would say that. For the past eighteen months he had made subtle and not so subtle hints to have her visit America. At the time, she'd been dealing with her volatile emotions and had declined his offers.

She melted into him, her lips pressed against his chest, muffling her voice. "Don't worry. I won't let this spoil my perception."

"Good."

"I'm happy to be here, Lucas." She closed her eyes, savoring how complete she felt enclosed in his arms. Soon it would be over and she'd be left cold. "I know that may seem strange with all that's going on, but I am happy to see you again."

He pressed a light kiss into her hair. The motion brought back another wave of bittersweet memories for her. He'd done that before and her heart ached. She took a step back, away from his warm and comforting body, and stared into his blue eyes.

His lips curled slightly. "Me too, Elena. Me too."

Chapter 16

Elena stepped through the kitchen door Lucas held open for her. They had finally returned home after dealing with the paperwork to ship Ivan's remains back to Russia. *Home.* How weird to think of Lucas's house as her home. She must be more tired than she thought. She would soon be finding herself on a plane with Dmitry heading back to the mother country.

The thought of returning to Russia should've made her happy. Back to her safe little world where she felt comfortable. Back to...what? For months, she'd been on the verge of making the move, only fear and panic holding her back. Her heart thumped, knowing soon she would have to confront Lucas and hear him out. Did she have the courage to hear him say what they had was now in the past? That she'd waited too long, and he'd grown tired of waiting? She swallowed around the lump in her throat.

"How's pizza sound?" Lucas's voice interrupted her increasingly worrying thoughts. She returned her focus to the present and noticed Dmitry had joined them.

"Delicious. I'm starving," she replied. Her stomach growled to prove her point. The last time she had a chance to grab something to eat was at breakfast. The day had gone fast and she'd been busy. After viewing Ivan, her body had rejected any idea of food and it wasn't until now that she felt hungry again.

Lucas nodded. "All right, I'll go order a couple for dinner."

He leaned his hip against the kitchen bench beside the wall mounted phone and lifted the handset while she listened to Dmitry reiterate his day's events.

"Here's what I got," he said. "The company that paid for the tickets was a dummy corporation. I did trace the credit card used back to the source…and get this. It's a government issued card. In fact, a DoD issued card."

She raised an eyebrow. "They used a government credit card? How stupid are they?"

Lucas shrugged. "Paper pushers, all tax-deducible when it's for work. This is America, after all."

Dmitry sat down, the motion tugging at his shirt, revealing his white bandage. She gasped, her eyes widening as she took in her brother's wound. "Oh my God, you're hurt. What happened?"

A wave of panic flowed through her before she tampered it down. Her hand trembled as her mind began imagining the worst. She had to get a grip. It was no good worrying about something that hadn't happened. Her brother was still alive. She refused to think of the alternative as she probed at his bandage and tried to determine if he had been injured anywhere else and wasn't telling her.

Her brother brushed off her concern. "It's just a little bullet wound."

"Just a...?" She huffed out a breath and muttered, "Men."

Her heartbeat returned to its regular rhythm, knowing Dmitry would only make light of his wound if it wasn't life threatening.

Her brother glared at Lucas as she fussed over him. "You said women dig a scar."

She turned narrowed eyes towards Lucas, then straightened her body and placed her hands on her hips. "You did, did you?"

***

Lucas grinned at Elena. He was used her mood swings by now, and nothing would ever make him fear her. She might send him to the dog house but he knew ways of making her forgive him. "I did. But I said *women*, Dmitry, not your older sister. That's a whole other kettle of fish."

"Relax, Elena. I'm fine." Dmitry batted Elena's hand away from him, sucking in a breath as she once more probed at his injury. "I also uncovered the name of the man who murdered Ivan."

Elena sat heavily in the chair she had recently vacated and stared at her brother.

"Good job. How'd you manage that?" Lucas asked, while waiting on hold to order the pizza.

119

"The age of technology, my computer illiterate friend," Dmitry said, then stepped back to the computer and sat down in the chair where he had spent the entire day.

After finalizing the order, Lucas hung up the phone and followed Elena and Dmitry.

"The warehouse didn't have any cameras, but the one several feet down did," Dmitry was saying to Elena when he reached them.

"The same camera that will be the final nail in your coffin."

Her reply had Dmitry wincing. "I take it things didn't go so good at Langley?"

Lucas stopped behind Elena and rubbed her tense shoulders. "It's a work in progress. So stay low," he warned. "The Secretary of Defense has a hard on for you. Show us what you found."

Nodding, Dmitry typed something into the computer. An image appeared on the screen of a couple of men exiting the warehouse rapidly.

"This was just after I escaped. I did get one slightly better shot of my mystery benefactor, and I was right when I figured he'd given me a fake name. I ran his picture through your DMV and got this—"

Dmitry brought up a copy of a Virginia driver's license, registered to Sean Michael Henry. Lucas retrieved his cell phone and pressed speed dial number four. "Is that address current?" he asked, while waiting for his call to be answered.

"I don't know. I'm having some trouble doing what I want. Your computer isn't exactly state of the art, Lucas. I'm working as fast as I can."

"Oh, here. I just remembered," Elena said, unzipping the carry-on bag she'd brought and pulling out a MacBook Pro that appeared to be brand new. She handed the computer to Dmitry, ignoring his glare which showed how annoyed he was that she hadn't thought of this before. Then she dug into her bag and retrieved the travel power convertor that would allow Dmitry to plug the Russian cord into the American outlet.

"Well, this should certainly help," Dmitry snapped.

"What?"

"Nothing," he replied grudgingly. "So just how bad is it?"

"Real bad. Keep out of sight, okay? I don't need anything else to happen to you."

"What about Ivan?"

Elena gave him a brief nod, telling him silently that everything had been sorted. Ivan was on his way back home to Russia. "I'm so sorry, Dmitry."

Dmitry stood and hugged his sister. "I know. I'm sorry too, Elena. I never wanted to involve you in this."

"I'm glad you did. Whenever you have problems, I'm supposed to help you out. Particularly problems like this one. Don't ever think not to tell me." Without warning, she slapped the back of his head.

"*Ow*, what was that for?"

Elena glared at him. "For not wanting to tell me. If Lucas hadn't called, I wouldn't have been here to help you, you chicken-shit."

Dmitry caught Lucas's gaze, sending a sarcastic

thank you glare his way. Lucas stared back at him, unfazed. For blood thirsty Russians, these two were kittens.

Forty minutes later, the three of them were finishing off one large supreme and one ham and pineapple pizza. "After dinner, I'll continue researching Sean Henry and why he wants Sundown. I'll also see how he came to be involved with the government," Dmitry said. "He doesn't seem the type to me. He had no problems shooting Ivan and had no remorse after."

Lucas thought about that. He knew many people within the government who would take a life for the security of the nation and those were men in low positions. No accounting what the big boys would do. "He's probably just a muscle man, you know, hired to keep the power player's hands clean."

Dmitry nodded, agreeing with him. "I'll dig deep. See if I can locate bank statements that can tell me who's footing the bills. For what he tried to pull off, he would need a man with deep pockets backing him. Maybe I'll get lucky and find the ring master in this circus."

"Just make sure you get some sleep, Dmitry," Elena said, speaking up for the first time since they'd sat down to dinner. "I don't like to see you so tired."

He rolled his eyes. "It will take as long as it does, Elena, but I promise I'll try my hardest to get some rest."

Chapter 17

Elena left Dmitry to his hacking. The less she knew, the better she felt. She'd never liked her brother's hobby or business venture—however he chose to see it. She'd always known it would lead him into trouble. He had an unnatural talent for delving into the world of cyberspace but she couldn't complain too much since it had saved her ass more than once.

She made her way down the hallway of Lucas's home. The house was predominately male. No woman had ever stayed long enough to leave a mark. Dark colors greeted her in chocolate, black, and forest green. She could see some work had been done recently. The smell of freshly painted walls assaulted her as she continued down the hall.

She felt Lucas's presence before she heard him. He wrapped his big hand around her arm and catapulted her into the nearest room which just happened to be his bedroom, then pinned her with his gaze, not allowing her to break contact. She swallowed nervously at the fierce look on his face, her mouth suddenly dry. He crossed his arms over his broad chest and leaned back against the closed bedroom door.

She was trapped.

"We're going to finish that talk we started in the car," he told her, and the expression on his face told her it was non-negotiable.

She let out a deep breath and sat on the edge of his massive king sized bed, creasing the black and white swirled design duvet. She wasn't looking forward to this talk. She shifted around, getting into a comfortable position buying herself some time while her incoherent thoughts flitted about her mind. She waited for him to start, not quite understanding why he was so mad at her if the look on his face was any indication. She glanced away, cowardly preparing herself for the confrontation.

He let out a deep sigh. "We shared something special at the airport, or at least I thought we did. Was I wrong?"

She jerked her head up to meet his eyes. Did he remember the airport? She sure did. That day had haunted her for eighteen long months.

"No, it's just—"

"What?" he interrupted. "Why have you stayed away? Have you changed your mind about us? If so, you should've said something instead of leaving me in the dark, wishing...wanting."

"Me? I haven't heard from you in over a month."

He blinked in surprise, then his face morphed into a frown. "The last time I called, I got the sense that I was crowding you so I thought I'd back off and give you the time I promised. You're important to me, Elena. I didn't want to screw up and push you away...or worse, have you run from me."

Her stomach twisted painfully. She'd never meant to give him that impression. She remembered the conversation. It had been after one of her panic attacks and she'd been a little distracted. Dread unfurled in her belly as she wondered if she was too late. She rushed to explain.

"I felt guilty at not being able to commit to you. I never meant to send you away. I don't want you to give up on me—on us."

He huffed out a frustrated breath. "I thought I could be patient with you, Elena, but my patience has run out. I want to know."

And he deserved to know how she felt. She wanted him to know. She hated the fact that since they'd first met she was the one holding back. First because of her allegiance to Nikolai and now from her own fear.

"I do love you, Lucas," she said softly, her eyes begging him to believe her. How she loved him. The insufferable man had gotten under her skin and imbedded himself so deeply within her that she would never be rid of him.

"Then why haven't you told me? Why haven't we been together all this time?"

The hurt on his face was almost her undoing. She chided herself, having been so wrapped up in her own feelings that she hadn't thought how he might take the situation. Exasperated, she threw up her hands. "Because I'm scared, okay?" When he looked like he was going to interrupt, she quickly continued, realizing how it must have sounded to him. "Not scared of us, Lucas. Never of that. I've only loved two men in my entire life and one was murdered. I don't want anything to happen to the other. I don't think I would survive that."

"Oh, Elena." He crossed the space of the room in three long strides and pulled her into his arms and held her tight, kissing the top of her head. "Nothing is going to happen to me."

She shook her head. "You can't promise me that."

"I can and I will. I love you so much, Elena."

She wrapped her arms around his neck and held onto him with all her strength. She kissed him hard with all the pent-up passion she had been harboring for the past eighteen months. She had let it grow and smolder and now she was ready to erupt. The electricity that had always been between them ignited and burned hot as it raced through her veins.

Her tongue stroked his as she took possession of his mouth, or was it he who took possession of hers? What did it matter? She was here with him, kissing him. Everything was finally right in the world as his large hands slid down her back, cupping her buttocks, pushing her body into his so she could feel his hardness on her belly. He wanted her. She kissed him again, moving closer to him, rubbing against his body, letting him know without words that she wanted him too.

He wrapped his arms around her waist and lifted her off the ground, settling her on the bed on her back. He pushed her thighs apart with his knee and knelt on one knee between them, his other foot still on the floor. Then he slowly lifted her blouse up and over her head, feasting his eyes on the creamy flesh he exposed. His flattened palm on her stomach made her shiver in desire. Small goosebumps appeared all over her skin. He kissed her again and again, letting his hands drift over her body, driving her wild as he pressed his hardness against her soft mound.

She quivered beneath him with passion as his hands settled on the waistband of her pants and undid them, pulling them down past her hips before discarding them. Now she only wore a lacy peach bra and matching panties. He gazed down at her, allowing his desire to show in the hard lines on his face. She felt her own desire course through her veins, warming her blood and causing her skin to flush as she realized how much the sight of her pleased him.

He removed his shirt and pants along with his boxers in record time. She heard the loud *clunk* sound as his gun holster hit the floor. Her lingerie shortly followed, and he settled between her thighs as he took one nipple in his mouth, caressing the other with his thumb so that the pink tip was hard and throbbing. He teased her mercilessly until she wildly bucked beneath him, raising her hips.

His hand slid down between the valley of her breasts and over her flat stomach before settling on her mound. Her breath hitched as he found her moist core. His tongue followed the path of his hand and she moaned at the first feel of his tongue in her most intimate of places. The world darkened as she thrashed her head against the already tousled sheets and she thought she might've passed out from sheer pleasure. Her thighs tightened around his head as he lapped at her, a shrill keening escaping her lips as he slowly tortured her, pushing her body higher and tauter without providing release.

She suddenly gasped, her body unwinding, shattering her consciousness as she came hard. She shivered and convulsed while he watched her. It should have disconcerted her but instead added to the sensual pleasure, his witnessing his effect on her.

He stroked her inner thighs with his tongue before sliding up her body to kiss her deeply, tasting herself on his lips. Once sated, she now throbbed with the need to feel him inside her. To join with him in the most basic and intimate ways. To show him without words how much she loved him so that he'd never question it again.

She felt his shaft pulsating against her damp mound, ready to explode. He was thick and long and smooth to the touch as she guided him to her. Perspiration dotted his forehead with the effort he took to hold himself back. Through clenched teeth he told her he didn't think he could control himself.

She shook her head. "I don't care, Lucas. I just want you."

She lifted her hips, the end of his engorged shaft grazing her silken entrance. A deep hunger unfurled in her belly, and he cursed under his breath, his control snapping. He grabbed hold of her hips and held her still as he entered her in one long trust. Elena moaned as he filled her up completely. She had never felt anything so right. This is what she'd always been waiting for without even knowing it.

She was connected to him in the most elemental way and never wanted him to leave. He swore savagely and began to withdraw, sliding from her body.

"No," she protested, tightening her legs around his waist to keep him inside her.

"I know," he said in a strangled tone. "But I'm not wearing a condom."

"That's okay. I'm protected. I trust you. Please don't leave. I need you, Lucas. Now and forever. Take me and don't hold back. I want every part of you."

He grinned rakishly. "My pleasure."

"Mine too." Her breathing hitched with excitement and her body tingled.

He moved within her, stimulating her already sensitive nerves, bringing her to orgasm within minutes. She shuddered beneath him and he followed her over as the muscles inside her gripped at him. He expanded within her, stretching her further before his release jetted into her.

He collapsed on top of her, struggling to breathe. With her imagination and wildest dreams, she still hadn't been anywhere close to conjuring up what it would be like when she and Lucas finally made love. She was in a state of euphoria, her entire being complacent.

He rolled off her and pulled her close. She stroked his chest as she waited for her heartbeat to return to its regular rhythm, feeling complete bliss in his arms. Something she'd not felt in a long time. Lucas made her feel alive again. She felt cherished in his arms and wondered how she could've ever thought he'd lost interest. Lucas was a man of his word.

"Good God, that was amazing."

"It was, wasn't it?" She suddenly had a thought and blushed. "I really hope Dmitry didn't hear any of that."

She hadn't once considered that her little brother was only down the hall—awake. She felt mortified that she had been so wrapped up with Lucas that she had totally forgotten Dmitry. Her face burned as she thought of how she'd cried out. She certainly hadn't been quiet.

"Relax, *sladkaya*," he intoned, calling her *sweetheart* in Russian. "I doubt your brother would notice the apocalypse outside his window unless something happened to the Internet."

Elena smiled. He knew Dmitry so well. He knew *her* so well. He looked deep into her eyes, having recently looked at every inch of her naked body. Her skin heated as she recalled the pleasure he'd built inside her and in her heart, as well. She wanted him again, more so than the first time. She began to wonder if she would ever have her fill of him.

"I promise the next time will last longer."

Had he been reading her mind? Her face heated at being caught, and Lucas leaned over and nibbled on her ear.

"And you know how I am with promises," he added in a husky voice.

Her heart beat sped up as his hands explored her once more, gliding sensually over her sensitive flesh. She turned her head to kiss him, and once more he kept his promise.

Chapter 18

Dmitry's wound throbbed, dull and incessant, a reminder that he was lucky to be alive, though hurting. Ivan was not. Not just his arm ached, but his heart too.

Anger and sorrow simultaneously burned and he fought against the volatile feelings, needing to remain clearheaded. Now wasn't the time to grieve. He couldn't allow his emotions to rule. He had to be cold and unfeeling like his nationality were often accused of being. Later, he could mourn Ivan, after he'd fulfilled his promise and avenged his friend.

He tilted his head and the bones cracked with the movement. He'd been sitting in the same position for too long.

He considered himself a smart man, but right now he felt like something important had been evading him. A pivotal piece of the puzzle, and it annoyed him. He didn't like the feeling, not having it very often. Something was very wrong. Something did not add up.

Why Sundown? That was the first question he

asked, and it was a good one. He didn't have an answer. The file had been classified, hidden deep inside the Pentagon's mainframe. Who knew about it? Surely it wasn't a long list, and it wouldn't be easy to obtain, but he was good at what he did and would find out.

It also helped keep his mind off whatever may be happening down the hall. He'd seen the determination in Lucas's eyes. Elena didn't stand a chance. He sat back in his seat, the hour long past midnight. He wondered briefly at their relationship, knowing there was more than passing interest between the two. Smoldering heat appeared between them whenever they got together. Dmitry hoped they worked it out. He didn't want to see either of them hurt. They both deserved a happy ending, at least for all the shit life had put them through.

He stared hard at the bright laptop screen. He certainly wasn't about to get his answers tonight, not with Sundown having a flag on the file. Anyone attempting to locate information on anything named Sundown would be getting a visit from the NSA. He would have to try something tomorrow, go to an unsecure location and download the information he wanted. He would have to be quick about it. The Department of Defense was not about to fool around. It was risky, but so was not doing anything.

He'd be crazy not to be scared, his future uncertain. Elena and Lucas could only protect him for so long. The rest would be up to him. He wouldn't let them down. It wasn't just about his life, but an entire country's freedom and safety. He couldn't step aside; it wasn't in his nature. He was the world's best hacker, and it was time to show them why he'd been bestowed the title.

The more Dmitry thought about it, the less sense it made. What good was stealing the security protocol for the country? There wasn't much you could do with it. The only thing that came to mind was money. Always money. The whole world was ruled by it.

With the threat of treason hanging heavily over his head, he continued to work.

Chapter 19

The boss glared at Sean, who hadn't been worth the trouble he'd gone through to acquire him. He had been a constant disappointment from the moment he'd hired him. The man was a thug, bought muscle. All he had to do was force the Russian to download Sundown and confirm once it had been finished, but the idiot had lost the entire goddamn protocol.

Fear blossomed inside him, his silk shirt clinging to his damp skin. The country was vulnerable. The entire defense force was on high alert, awaiting the possibility of attack. He channeled his fear into anger and focused it on Sean, who it appeared couldn't follow a directive without monumentally fucking up.

"I just got word that Elena Ivanova is in Washington," the boss said. "She met with SAC Fitzgibbon at Langley this morning along with Secretary Mann of the Pentagon. Apparently, the woman has friends in high places."

Something his subordinate had neglected to

mention. If he'd known Dmitry Ivanov was related to a woman who worked for Russian intelligence, he never would've allowed Sean to hire him. He didn't like surprises, but maybe he could use this to his advantage.

"I'm well aware. I'm close to retrieving the file," Sean replied. "I've learned Ivanova has a relationship with an agent here in the States, a Lucas Gates. I believe that she is staying with him and that her brother is with them."

He let out a frustrated sigh. "This was not supposed to happen. Sundown was not supposed to be endangered."

He hadn't wanted to compromise the protocol, only wanted the paper-pushers in the White House to see how wrong they were, and now everything was fucked. The entire system had escaped into the void, available to anyone with the know-how.

He only hoped Dmitry Ivanov was as good as he had proved so far. He knew the man didn't want to jeopardize the country's defenses. From what Sean had said, Ivanov had recognized the IP address and had to be forced to retrieve the file. He sounded like a decent man; it was a shame to have to involve him in this issue, but something had to be done. The country was not secure, and wouldn't be until the men at the top saw it for themselves.

This wasn't how he had planned it, but nothing could change it now. Now he had to retrieve Sundown from wherever Ivanov had sent the files, and replace it back in the Pentagon's mainframe. Only then would he be safe from prosecution.

It was a shame the same couldn't be said for the

Russian, but certain sacrifices were necessary and his reputation and position were more valuable than one man's life.

No one must know that it was he who had arranged the entire thing.

Chapter 20

Elena inhaled the clean scent of a man—her man. She could have been blind and would still be able to pick Lucas out of a crowd. She drowsily opened her eyes and looked up into his brilliant blue ones, the skin around the sockets crinkling, showing his age as he smiled down at her. With slightly damp hair, dressed in a light grey suit and blue shirt he looked downright edible. She licked her lips and his eyes followed her tongue. Her body warmed, desire coursing through her as if she had become some horny hormonal time bomb.

"I've got to go into work but you stay here and help Dmitry, all right? I'll be home as soon as I can."

She nodded her understanding, her mind a riot of erotic memories of the previous night. Lucas leaned down and gave her a kiss that if she ended up with Alzheimer's in her old age, it would be the one thing she would remember with crystal clear clarity.

He sent her a sexy grin before picking up his keys from the bed side table and leaving her with her thoughts. She climbed out of bed, pulling on Lucas's shirt that had been left discarded on the floor and made her way to the kitchen. Her body was slightly sore from the previous evening's activities. It had been over two years since she had last made love and her inner muscles were now protesting that fact. She smiled. Lucas certainly hadn't gone easy on her just as she hadn't with him.

She looked about the kitchen. The carafe was empty and had been for some time. She frowned when she couldn't see any signs of Dmitry and assumed he had finally relented and had gone to bed. Her brother was far too used to staying awake all night, streamlining caffeine. She had told him more than once she worried about it. It certainly wasn't good for him but he'd yet to change his nighttime habits.

She'd begun preparing the coffee maker for another batch when a piece of paper on the kitchen table caught her eye. Picking it up, she recognized Dmitry's handwriting. The letter had been written in Russian. Either by habit or because he was paranoid, she didn't know. She quickly read through his letter telling her he had gone to the library to do some research he couldn't risk doing at Lucas's.

She shook her head. *Be safe, Dmitry, and for goodness sake keep your head down.*

He was taking a huge risk, and had she been around when the decision was made, she would've fought to keep him from going. Which was probably why he had snuck out while she was sleeping, the little shit.

She crumpled up the letter and threw it in the bin, then finished loading the coffee maker and pressed the start button before retracing her steps back down the hall towards the bathroom. She let the almost burning hot water of the shower beat down on her shoulders and back, loosening the tension that she hadn't realized was there, and washed away the dried perspiration left over from the night before. She almost moaned in delight as the water performed miracles on her sore muscles.

Several wonderful minutes later, she climbed out of the shower and dried herself off, dressing in her favorite worn pair of jeans. She added a peach blouse and put on her sneakers, brushed her teeth and hair before exiting the bathroom, and decided it was time for her morning coffee. The machine should have finished making the pot by now.

She poured the coffee into a mug with the CIA emblem and took a sip. She felt the caffeine begin to take effect as it zinged through her bloodstream. She was halfway through the mug when she heard a car pull into Lucas's driveway. She stood, thinking it was Dmitry, and walked towards the kitchen door that led out to the garden which she'd learned was Lucas's preferred entrance. She saw the shadowed figure on the opposite side and stiffened, knowing immediately that it wasn't her brother. The silhouette of the man on the other side of the door didn't match him or Lucas. Her suspicion was proven correct when she heard the scraping sound of a small tool being forced into the locking mechanism on the door.

She backed away toward Lucas's bedroom. She

remembered seeing him lock away his weapon there. She went straight to his closet and found the safe, the code still imprinted into the computer. Opening the safe, she sighed in relief at the sight of an eight shot revolver with a black handle, then checked to make sure it was loaded before slowly returning to the kitchen where the man continued working on Lucas's lock.

She reacquainted herself with the weapon, holding the familiar weight in her hand, and breathed slowly to avoid panicking. She had to trust herself; one wrong move could prove disastrous for her and for the man on the other side of the door. Her heart thumped in her chest and she took a moment to calm herself. Panicking never helped anyone, and while she didn't believe it, it could be very well be a common burglar.

They certainly picked the wrong house, she thought, gripping the handle firmly and resting her finger against the trigger guard.

She lifted the revolver and aimed toward the door as it opened. The man stepped through, his eyes widening in surprise at the sight of her with the gun.

"Who are you?" she asked.

The man before her was no common burglar. He was clean-shaven and she could see the outline of his weapon under his shirt. His eyes held a shrewd intelligence that sent a shiver down her spine.

"Relax, honey. It's all good. No need to be pointing that gun at me."

His vocabulary made him seem American lower class, not college educated. If she had to guess she'd say he'd barely finished high school, but she wouldn't underestimate him. She'd met men like him in the past and knew not to turn her back on them. His gaze drifted up and down her body in a way that made her want to run to the nearest toilet and throw up. She glared at him, moving the sight of the gun lower until it was pointing at the zipper on his pants.

"Hey," he immediately covered the area with his hands as if this would stop a bullet. "Watch where you're pointing that thing."

"Remove your weapon," she said, her tone telling him she would shoot if necessary.

"What weapon?"

"I'm not stupid. Remove it or I will remove a part of you. One you will most certainly miss."

His eyes widened further as he stared at her and gauged that she wasn't kidding. She made sure he understood that perfectly well. He moved slowly, removing his gun from the waistband of his pants with two fingers. He tossed the pistol to the ground away from his reach.

She watched as he briefly looked past her. She felt the presence behind her and acted too late. She didn't have a chance to swing around before the second intruder had his weapon digging into her back in direct line with her kidney. If he pulled the trigger she was dead. He had snuck up behind her. The man could have been a ghost. She'd not heard him, not one squeak of a floorboard or one exhale of breath.

The man stepped forward and she studied his face, her fear slowing down time, allowing her to process everything around her. She stiffened when she recognized him from the security feed Dmitry had found. This was the man who'd shot Ivan and tried to kill Dmitry. She barely suppressed the snarl that threatened to escape her mouth.

How had they found her? Her mind gave her the simplest answer. They'd followed her and Lucas from the morgue.

The man relieved her of the gun before pointing it back at her. Like his friend didn't already have a good enough hold over her. She tried to get a look at the man behind her but he was a professional and kept his face hidden from view.

"When you aim a gun, young lady, be prepared to fire it," the man behind her lectured smugly. She could hear the age and wealth of experience in his voice.

Bastard. She had no compunctions about firing a weapon. In fact she had shot and killed a man just two years ago in self-defense. The man had been a terrorist and would have shot Lucas had she not intervened. She just wanted to avoid an international incident, and didn't fancy spending her time in any American prisons.

"Think you can handle it from here, Henry, or would you like me to hold your hand?" the man behind her asked Ivan's killer. Using names and not bothering to conceal their identities…this was not good. Not one fucking bit. Her heart leapt as panic rose within her.

Sean's eyes narrowed, his face turning red. Elena could see he wanted to tell the man behind her where to go, that or shoot him, but he must be quite powerful or just plain scary. His lips tightened, thinning as he nodded curtly. She felt the pressure of the gun alleviate from her back and she was then pushed toward Sean Henry. He grabbed her hands as she came close to him. His entire focus on his next step, she used his lack of concentration against him, knocking him off balance and into the island bench nearby. His body rammed hard into the ninety degree angle corner of the bench and his cry of pain almost deafened her as she made a leap for Lucas's revolver.

The second man came up behind her and grabbed her hair, yanking her head backwards until she was looking up into his hard angry eyes. Her palm closed around the butt of the gun. She bit down hard on her bottom lip to stifle the gasp of pain, unwilling to give the man any satisfaction, and glared up at him, ignoring the metallic tang of blood in her mouth as her teeth cut the soft tissue of her lips.

Raising the revolver, she brought it down hard over the man's head. His breath hissed out and he pulled tighter on her hair, bringing her closer to him, his free hand applying pressure on her wrist until she dropped Lucas's gun once more.

Limping, Sean reached inside his pocket and brought up a small black object. She struggled futilely against the second man's strong hold as his arm wrapped around her chest, capturing her flailing arms and pinning them down.

For a moment she thought she should know him, that she had seen him somewhere before. He looked so familiar as if she knew him or at least knew *of* him. No memory was forthcoming. The man had obviously been in the army at some point, her panicked mind interpreting his efficient actions, as he applied force against certain pressure points on her body that had her unwillingly relenting to him.

"Hurry up, Henry, this one's a real fighter."

Sean nodded as he came at her while simultaneously powering what she now recognized as a taser. He sent a dark look toward her as moved closer, telling her that he would enjoy the pain he inflicted on her. She steeled herself against the pain she knew was coming, just as he pressed the device hard against her hip, allowing for no mistakes.

A bolt of electricity zinged through her and this time she couldn't stifle the cry of agony. She attempted to dislodge him by throwing her head left and right but he only pressed harder almost fracturing her hip bone in the process. The man behind her tightened his grip painfully warning her silently.

She jerked from the jolt and darkness invaded her vision. She tried to shake it off, to keep fighting but her body began to feel heavy and sluggish. She soon found she could barely move her arms. The man who looked so familiar stared down at her, watching as she fell unconscious.

Chapter 21

Lucas sauntered into Jim's office. The man sat behind his desk reading through his emails. He hadn't wanted to leave Elena, more than willing to crawl back into bed with her, but he had to work. He hadn't been prepared for her impromptu visit.

Once the situation with Dmitry stabilized, he would ask for a couple days off to sweet-talk her into staying. He hoped after last night groveling wouldn't be necessary, though he was prepared to do or say anything. He needed her in his life. Her mere presence filled him with love and happiness. Despite Dmitry's circumstances, Elena walking through his door was the best day of his life.

He was one step closer to having everything he could ever want.

His boss looked up as he stepped close and swiveled his chair, turning it toward the printer where he picked up a fresh piece of paper off the feeder and handed it to Lucas.

"Here's the information you requested about Sean Michael Henry, hot off the press. I won't ask you how you came about this name. I doubt if it just fell out of the sky."

Lucas nodded. "Good idea. Thanks, Jim."

James waved a hand in dismissal. "I didn't do it for you, Lucas, you know that. I like Elena. Have since the day I first spoke with her and I'm sure I will like this Dmitry as well when I eventually meet him. One hell of a family, no doubt."

He quickly skimmed what the tech guys downstairs had found on Sean Henry. The address was the same as the one on his driver's license. He read the list of charges and arrests on his rap sheet, including several small stints in a federal prison.

"I know this goes without saying but I'll say it anyway. He's not the type of man you want hanging around or sniffing about," Fitzgibbon continued as he read. "You may want to let your answering machine know."

Lucas didn't need to be told twice. He already had his phone out and was dialing his house number before James had finished speaking. He listened to it ring before his answering machine picked up. Elena was probably screening his calls. He spoke into the machine, asking for her to pick up. After a few seconds, when it was clear neither Elena nor Dmitry were going to answer, he hung up and tried the number again.

He didn't like this. After reading Henry's file, his discomfort only increased. Sean Henry wasn't the type of man he'd call intelligent. There was someone out there making the decisions, someone with brains. Henry was hired muscle, and dangerous muscle at that. He heard the machine pick up again and swore eloquently.

Where the hell are Dmitry and Elena?

Chapter 22

Dmitry made his way through the throng of researchers and visitors and took a seat in an isolated area of the circular reading room beneath the pale blue domed ceiling of the Library of Congress. He'd chosen the library for its grand size and because he could easily blend in and get lost in the crowd, should there be a need.

He pulled out Elena's laptop from his backpack and hooked it up to the library's free Wi-Fi. He accessed the Internet, bringing up the program he had created the night before. One that would confuse any tracers for a small period of time. It wasn't the best, but it would do. He needed all the help he could get. He only had one chance at collecting the information he desired and knew that what he was after would provide the answer and bring about the proof of his innocence.

He started the program. Once a trace was detected, the software would send the technical operator a series of incorrect locations all around the world. It would only last five minutes—four if the tech was good—before his real location was discovered.

Dmitry made himself comfortable, looking about the reading room. No one was paying him any special attention so he continued typing in the commands.

Time to get this party started.

He once more accessed the Pentagon's mainframe. The security was tighter but still ineffectual against him. He brought up the administrator's profile he had created before under GreyHat01, somewhat surprised it hadn't been found and deleted, and made his way deep into the internal data banks and typed Sundown into a search box. He added a few other key words such as *implement* and *protocol* for good measure, in case Sundown alone wouldn't give him the specific results.

He prayed he would find what he was looking for since he risked a lot to do so. Sifting quickly through useless search results, he was left with four pages of information. He skimmed through each of the pages before finding what he was after on the third: a complete list of those involved in the inception of Sundown from design to execution. He sent the data to his iPhone knowing he would barely have enough time to get out of the building before the agents arrived.

Returning his fingers to the keyboard, he searched through cyberspace and entered the dark web where the stain of humanity roamed. He didn't have much time—two minutes, tops—before he had to get out of there. He had no doubt whatsoever that the men with guns were on their way here now.

Money. It is always about the bloody money.

As they said in the movies, follow the money. They were right.

He found what he was looking for, briefly skimming over the words on the page, and absorbing the information before closing down the laptop and returning it to the backpack. Knowing what he did now, he had something to bargain with—something other than Sundown. He felt a lot better, almost like normal again. Rising calmly, as if he had all the time in the world, he made his way between the arched desks and toward the door.

He descended three sets of staircases to the street and crossed the road to the small park and sat down on a bench that looked out toward the library. He watched as three black government issued vehicles pulled up outside, red and blue lights flashing within the grilles.

Accessing his phone, he brought up the downloaded material. He scrolled through the pictures of the people privy to Sundown. Distinguished looking men peered back at him, one of who had organized the theft of a highly classified document. He listened to the shouts of the team of government agents swarming over the steps of the library as he read the brief bios of the men. None of them sounded like the person he would have thought was involved, but how could he be sure? Human nature couldn't be measured.

His cell phone vibrated and the caller ID showed Lucas calling. He hoped he had good news.

"Where are you?" Lucas demanded, his voice

brimming with worry.

Oh God, what now?

"At the library."

Lucas let out a deep breath. "Is Elena with you?"

"No. Why?"

If anyone should know where Elena had gone, it was Lucas. The two were practically joined at the hip now. He shuddered at the thought that popped inside his head. There were just certain things a brother shouldn't think about when it included his sister.

"I just got home, and when I got here, the kitchen door was open and it looks like there was a struggle. They've got her, Dmitry. The son-of-a-bitches have her."

Something thudded loudly. He could practically feel the anger vibrating off every word Lucas spoke. If they couldn't find Elena, there was only one viable reason, and that was not a pleasant thought. He gulped, his stomach churning, not wanting to think about what Henry and his men could be doing to his sister. He tried to clear his head and took a deep breath in an attempt to calm himself.

"They won't hurt her," he said, not quite believing it. "Not while I'm still at large, at least. They want me, not her." His heart hurt knowing she was in danger.

"These people won't stop at anything to get you to do what they want you. Just look at your friend Ivan."

Dmitry heard a car door slam shut right before the engine caught.

"Which library are you at?" Lucas asked.

"Congress. Outside the main entrance to the Thomas Jefferson Building."

"What are you doing?" Lucas started, before exhaling deeply. "Never mind. You can tell me when I get there. Stay where you are. I'm coming to get you."

Chapter 23

She was floating in a sea of ecstasy. Her entire body felt as weightless as a feather. She felt giddy— almost as if she was drunk. Giggles bubbled up from inside her like champagne. It was almost as if she was having an out of body experience and wondered if at any time would she float above her body and look down at herself.

She arched her back as she felt his tongue glide up her body starting at her belly button and moving up her neck before it turned into a delectable kiss. She tasted him and breathed his masculine scent into her. Her toes curled. Her breath hitched and she struggled to breathe. She had never felt this way before. This was as close to heaven as she could get while she was still alive—and she was alive.

So very alive. Every nerve screamed as he touched her. His fingers left scorching marks in their wake. She thought she would be burned up by sheer pleasure. She watched his face as he leaned over her. His eyes dark with passion as he kissed her again and again.

153

"Lucas," she said softly, reaching out to him. Her eyelids were heavy. She found herself unable to open them and could smell the tangy scent of men's body odor. She struggled to move. Her body felt weighted down, but she could have sworn there was nothing on top of her.

They moved rapidly along a road. The cacophony of heavy traffic surrounded her. Honking horns, tires screeching and men cursing. The car went over a pothole and jarred her. Pain raced up the length of her arm and darkness swam around her as she attempted to fight it off.

"Lucas," she whispered again, her head moving back and forward slightly as she fought to regain complete consciousness.

"Looks like someone is waking up." A man spoke, and she guessed he sat in the front of the car. The voice sounded familiar to her foggy brain. Her head pounded and her throat was sore. What the hell happened to her and why did she feel so tired?

She tried to open her eyes again and failed. Exhausted from the effort, she moved her head slightly to alleviate the ache inside. The sun against her face heated her skin.

Good. Maybe I haven't been out that long. Not unless it was the next day and she had slept through the night.

"Better move quickly," the man's companion said. "I don't want to have to fight the bitch again."

Another familiar voice. Her sluggish mind tried desperately to come to an answer. Where was she and how did she get here? Why couldn't she remember and why did she feel so heavy? Elena tried to move her hands and found them to be bound together. She moved her body and felt a tingling numbness and her memory came rushing back. She'd been alone at Lucas's when two men had broken in, and she fought them only to fail.

The sound of a cell phone camera taking a photo penetrated the fogginess. She had no doubts as to the subject.

"If she gives us any more trouble we'll just give her another shot of the taser," the first man said.

That explained her current circumstance. The bastards had knocked her unconscious. She would have to pay them back for that later once she got to her feet and wasn't feeling so nauseous.

She had no idea where she was or where she was going. The only consolation she had was that she knew the men wanted Dmitry and not her; she was just a means to an end. She hoped they weren't stupid enough to harm her, at least not until they had Dmitry.

"I'd rather just shoot the bitch if she tries anything. Hear that, bitch? Don't you go doing something stupid, all right?"

Her foggy brain placed the sound of his voice. Dmitry's benefactor. The man who'd killed Ivan. The pieces she had been missing clicked back into place.

Elena ignored the man. She would have to be dumb to promise something so ridiculous. She would make as much trouble as she could to escape before they got their hands on her little brother. She had begun entertaining some rather painful moves against her captors, and she would enjoy every single one.

"Just call Ivanov," the first man said. She remembered him as being an older gentleman. A man who had held himself with power, a man she knew she should recognize.

The sound of the cell phone's buttons being pressed filled the small space. The hair on her arms stood at attention as she heard the voice on the other end answer.

Chapter 24

Dmitry followed Lucas closely as he stormed into the office at Langley. An older man glanced up in surprise, his gaze falling on him after sweeping over Lucas's infuriated expression. His gut clenched as anxiety ate away at him. This was the last place he wanted to be, but Elena's well-being was on the line so he pushed aside his fears. Well, almost—his hands shook slightly as he waited for handcuffs to be tightened around his wrists, though rationally he knew that wasn't about to happen. Lucas wouldn't have brought him to the heart of the CIA if that had been a concern, and so far no one had attempted to take him into custody.

It was bigger than him now. Sean Henry had made a grave mistake. No one hurt his sister and walked away. If they wanted a fight, they'd gotten one. Neither he nor Lucas would ever back down.

"I'm not bringing him in," Lucas said as Dmitry closed the door behind him.

He caught the older man's gaze, expression blank, despite the overwhelming urge to squirm beneath his commanding presence.

The man leaned back in his chair. "I didn't even entertain the thought. I know you too well, my friend. Why is he here? If you're looking for a safe house, might I suggest another location?" He frowned, his jovial attitude dissipating as the anger radiating off Lucas's body seemed to reach him. Dmitry knew the agony Lucas experienced because he felt the same. He was a man being torn apart. "What's happened?"

"The bastards have Elena," Lucas replied, speaking through a clenched jaw as he tried to keep his temper in check, his expression turning savage. There was no doubt in his mind that when Lucas found the men holding the love of his life, he would make them beg for mercy.

"What?" The older man exploded in fury. "When did this happen?"

"Sometime this morning." Lucas turned to him. "Dmitry, get on Jim's computer and locate her cell phone GPS. Use his access to get a fixed satellite position. I want to know exactly where she is."

Jim raised his eyebrows but didn't comment. There would be no arguing or bargaining with Lucas at the moment.

Dmitry moved to stand beside Jim, then leaned over him and readjusted the keyboard to accommodate his position.

"Excuse me," he said as he began to pull up a satellite search program. He typed in Jim's user name and password without having to ask for them.

"Jesus Christ," Lucas's boss muttered, realizing Dmitry had cracked the code in less than two minutes. "Certifiably dangerous is what you are, son. Thank goodness you're one of the good guys."

He didn't have time to express what Jim's words meant to him, the knowledge he had another ally, but his relief was almost euphoric, and his body sagged as his knees weakened. One thought of Elena had the tension returning.

He deftly entered his sister's cell phone number in the allotted field. A red box appeared on screen saying '***No Hits Found.***' He turned to peer over his shoulder at Lucas. "It's not currently turned on. The last place it was on, she was right here."

"Right," Lucas said. "Elena checked her messages here before speaking briefly with Mishkin yesterday. What about before that?"

Dmitry once more consulted the map before him on the computer screen. He hit a few keys before answering. "The GPS stops there. On and off within ten minutes, previous location was Moscow. She would have turned it off for the flight." The computer binged, alerting them to a new development. "Whoa, wait a sec, it just came back on."

The phone was in transit, moving fast along the Beltway heading north. Dmitry barely had time to lock the satellite onto the phone before his cell began to ring. He pulled it out of his pocket and looked at the caller ID. Elena. He answered the call, putting it on speaker.

"Elena?"

"Mr. Ivanov, good to finally get a hold of you," the caller said. Dmitry recognized the voice as the man who had shot Ivan.

"Sean Henry?"

"Shit, you are good," the man said before his voice turned hard. "Now, listen up here, comrade. I'm sending you a photo. Do as I say or another will follow, one that will be less pleasant."

His phone vibrated as the photo arrived. He clicked on the screen of his iPhone to open the message and immediately wished he hadn't. He ground his teeth together as the picture appeared on his cell screen. Elena was laying unconscious on the backseat of a car, her face pale, and he could see the beginning of a bruise on her throat.

Lucas looked over his shoulder at the photo and his face contorted with rage. He tried to snatch the phone away from him, but Dmitry moved away out of his reach. Lucas looked downright homicidal, and at that moment, Dmitry knew without a doubt that his friend loved Elena. It was more than just a roll in the sack for him. He already knew she loved him more than anything—maybe even more than Nikolai. It had almost killed her when Lucas had flown home, yet she took pains not to show it. He only hoped they got their chance at happily ever after.

"If you hurt her, I will find you, Henry, and inflict the most painful torture techniques known to man on you. Remember, I'm Russian, so I know all the good ones. That's why you wanted me, right, because of my nationality? God help you if you don't release my sister."

"Touching, really," Sean answered snidely. "It all comes down to you, comrade. You meet my man out in front of the Lincoln Memorial in half an hour—alone—and follow his instructions, and I promise I won't hurt your sister. Don't do as I say, and I'll find some men who'll really have some fun with her. She is quite beautiful, you know."

Lucas made another attempt to get the phone. Dmitry sidestepped, putting Jim between him and Lucas. He wondered how much the man knew. Was he aware that the house he took Elena from belonged to a CIA Agent? If so, he was overly confident. Only he'd miscalculated. Lucas would do anything to ensure Elena's safety. Hadn't he proved that when he'd taken on Dmitry? It was all over for Sean. He just didn't know it yet. There was no place he could hide that Dmitry wouldn't find him.

"I'll play nice," he told Sean.

"Good to hear, comrade. See you soon. Oh, and no tricks, you hear?"

No, not while you have the upper hand. Once we're on even ground, though, you'd better watch out.

"No tricks."

He wasn't about to risk Elena's well-being. Not for anything, including the security of a nation. He would gladly hand Sundown over on a silver platter if it meant Elena went free and unharmed. He would fix what was broke later. He'd devise a new protocol if he had to. One that would actually be safe and he wouldn't go and advertise it on the mainframe, either.

Idiots. Had they no idea that cyberspace is one big shopping ground?

Dmitry hit the *end call* button and looked once again at the photo of Elena. Anger bubbled to the surface when he thought of her lying there helpless, bound and hurt. He took a steadying breath and dropped his phone down on the desk.

Lucas erupted, no longer able to keep his thoughts inside his head. "Dmitry, I'm not letting you go into this alone. Not while yours and Elena's lives are at stake."

"You don't have much of a choice, Lucas," Jim countered.

"We don't have much time. I have to be there in thirty minutes, so unless you can come up with a better plan that won't get Elena killed in that time, I'm going."

Lucas nodded. "Here." He held out his cell. "We'll track you through the GPS."

"Too big. It'll be the first thing they'll ask for," Jim said.

In a moment of sudden inspiration, Dmitry took his own cell phone and threw it hard against the floor, the back splitting away from the cracked screen. He bent down, retrieved the phone and tore the back completely away and picked out what he wanted—the GPS chip that was smaller than his thumbnail. He moved back to the computer, typing commands, including the numerical code printed on the GPS device that he'd pulled from the phone. Lucas and Jim watched, speechless.

"Okay, this works just like the cell thing, okay? But instead it looks for the chip, not the phone." He placed the GPS chip into the front right hand pocket of his jeans. "Don't touch anything, and you can't fuck it up."

"I take offense to that," Jim said.

"Charge me later. Add it to my never ending list. Don't follow me and don't do a thing to risk Elena. I mean it. Catching the bad guys isn't worth her life. I'll bring her back, Lucas, I promise."

Lucas placed a hand on his shoulder and squeezed. "I know. She means the world to both of us. We can't afford to lose her."

***

Twenty-five minutes later, Dmitry parked Lucas's car near the Lincoln Memorial. His long strides easily shortened the distance until he stood on the stairs leading to the monument, staring out at the Potomac.

He crossed his arms over his chest and waited. Tourists milled around, giving him a wide berth. Not that he blamed them. He knew what he must look like, with his dark Ray-Bans covering his eyes, his stiff countenance. Children squealed excitedly, racing past, not sensing the danger he represented. He wanted to be a tourist, too, exploring this magnificent city but first he had a sister and country to save.

A vehicle revved nearby, the choking exhaust catching his attention. A man stood beside a 1979 beige Dodge Aspen. Just his luck, the man glaring at him was the hired muscle he'd fought at the warehouse. He wore jeans, dark motorcycle boots, and a stained wife beater tank top which was in desperate need of a wash. The bulge of a weapon was visible beneath his shirt. His large muscles were decorated with tattoos running the length of

163

his arms, and his eyes were hidden behind dark tinted sunglasses—most likely to dim the light against his damaged corneas. The man had gotten what he deserved.

When he reached the vehicle, the man, his face grim, opened the back door of the car, and indicated without words for Dmitry to climb in. He waited briefly, most likely searching the area for back-up, then got in beside him.

The driver, a man who lacked the same social and hygiene skills as the hired muscle, put the Dodge in gear and merged into the traffic. They rode in silence, listening to the sounds of the cars around them. They travelled roughly three miles down the road before the car veered off down an exit ramp and pulled into the parking lot of a 7-Eleven, and parked beside a set of filthy looking bathrooms.

The man looked at Dmitry and said, "Come on."

Nervous, he followed without complaint, noting the man carried a plastic Wal-Mart bag. They walked up to the men's restroom, and the man waited for Dmitry to precede him. He watched Dmitry like a hawk watching his prey, most likely waiting for a reason to strike at him. His employer had probably given him a no touching command—can't break the fingers that would bring them Sundown, after all. Dmitry stepped inside and turned around to face the hired muscle, his hair again pulled back in a ponytail, waiting for the next set of instructions.

"Strip," Ponytail said.

He paused, disbelieving what he heard. The man

glared at him. "I said strip, you commie bastard."

"You know you really should learn to be more P.C. I'm not a communist, nor have I ever been. I may be Russian, and you call me that or Dmitry, but you call me a commie again, Ponytail, and we'll have a problem," he said as he began removing his clothes.

"Whatever," Ponytail said.

Let the man get his jollies by watching him undress. He had never been ashamed or embarrassed by his body. Not that he any reason to be; his body hard from working out at a gym, his muscles well-defined. He might not be as strong as Ponytail, but he was faster and smarter. Brains often beat brawn. It was just a matter of timing.

Once he was naked, Ponytail gave his body a cursory look before handing him a set of clean clothes he had retrieved from the Wal-Mart bag. Dmitry took the black sweat pants and Washington Redskins hooded jumper and repressed a violent shudder. If he had to die, the last thing he wanted to be wearing was sweats. And, Redskins? Had he not suffered enough?

Dressing quickly, he glanced at his discarded clothing. He should've anticipated they'd make him change. He'd merely been expecting a pat down. Returning to the car, his wrists were promptly bound in shiny new stainless steel handcuffs. He guessed now that they knew he had no weapon, and wasn't wired, with no way to contact anyone, he could be taken to see Elena.

Chapter 25

They drove for another forty minutes to a neat and quiet suburb. The houses all looked like something that would grace the glossy cover of a homes and gardens magazine. Not one leaf marred the pristine lawns of the pompous pricks who resided in the large houses that lined the street. He was led up the path to the front door and pushed not so gently inside.

Dmitry snarled as he took in his surroundings. The décor was expensive and new, the walls decorated with artistic prints that one would have to be insane to own. A Persian rug lay between two stylish sofas, covered in plush cushions. To his left, a desk and computer stood, and in the center of the room, silently fuming and sitting on a kitchen chair, was Elena. Her hands, like his, were handcuffed in front of her. She stopped glaring at her captors when she spotted him and worry furrowed her brow before quickly turning her fear back into anger.

She was all right—for the time being, at least. Whoever decided to mess with her at the moment would have some protruding part of their anatomy removed painfully, judging by the death glares she sent toward Sean's goons. Elena had not taken being kidnapped and held against her will lightly. Dmitry could see she was buying time, trying to come up with a decent plan to escape with both their lives intact—all while planning the deaths or maiming of the burly lackey goons.

"Elena," Dmitry said, moving toward her only to be blocked by another muscular man with a tattoo of a dragon down the right hand side of his face.

"Dmitry, so good to see you," Sean Henry said as he came into sight. "You have caused me a great deal of trouble. My boss wasn't very forgiving. He wants the file, you see, and you have inconvenienced him terribly."

He resisted the urge to roll his eyes. The man was acting like he was part of a gangster movie.

"Yeah, I'm real broken up about that," he said, making sure Sean could hear the lack of interest in his tone.

Sean narrowed his eyes and hit Dmitry hard in the stomach, momentarily winding him. He heard Elena anxiously calling out his name, wanting to know if he was all right. He listened as she swore and cursed in Russian. The woman had a sailor's mouth—words *he* didn't even say out loud. She certainly hadn't learnt them from him.

Sean cracked his knuckles. "Don't smart ass me."

Dmitry straightened his body, standing up to his full height and looked the murdering bastard in the eyes. He almost smiled when the other man

167

shivered from the frightening look he knew was in his cool grey eyes, promising things he would do to the man had his wrists not been restrained in handcuffs.

"You hit like a girl, Sean," he said, "and you had to do it when I was cuffed, so what does that tell you? You're a spineless coward and you will get your comeuppance. I will make sure of it."

Sean made another fist, determined to hit him again, when the boss made his entrance. The man commanded attention. He was an older gentleman of about fifty, his hair grey and receding, his eyes a dark brown. Dmitry could tell he was accustomed to loyalty and authority.

Dmitry recognized power when he saw it, guessing he'd been in the Armed Forces—a man whose rank had been high at one time. Anyone who tried to fuck him over had to be either downright stupid or desperate.

He also looked very familiar. He searched his mind for the answer, but none was forthcoming. Either way, it wasn't something he would waste energy on.

Sean let his fist drop and shoved Dmitry forward, closer to his boss. The older man surveyed Dmitry as if he was a slab of meat, appearing pleased at the gift he'd been given.

"Dmitry Ivanov in the flesh. It is a real shame it had to go down like this, my friend. You could have been extremely useful to the country, otherwise. I do not wish to hurt you or your sister," the man added, glancing over at Elena. He spoke as if he'd only just remembered that he had kidnapped her.

"So, if you please, retrieve Sundown and return it to me."

Dmitry snorted. "It was never yours to begin with, and either way we're dead. I've seen the way you do business...and they call us Russians cold. I'm not about to make your life easier just so I can be killed after I've outlived my usefulness. I'm not that stupid."

The boss gave him a small smile. "You have balls, Dmitry. It's a shame we can't work together. We are, after all, on the same side."

"Which is precisely why I'm handcuffed here against my will," Elena said sarcastically.

The boss looked at her once more. "All unfortunate circumstances, Agent Ivanova, I assure you. It pains me to see such a fine, loyal agent of the SVR in such a position, but I'm afraid my priorities are not with you. I must have Sundown back."

He knew Elena was SVR and he had taken her from a CIA agent's house. This man was not fucking shy, that was for sure. He had no doubt he would do just about anything he wanted and the worse bit was that he could and would get away with it.

"And Ivan Anisimov, what is he, a causality of war?" Dmitry asked, his voice steely. Just thinking about Ivan's tragic ending made him extremely pissed off. It had been a meaningless waste. "Or was he just another unfortunate circumstance?" Dmitry added, staring hard at the man, not allowing him to break eye contact.

He had to give him some credit. He didn't shiver

or back down like others had done, including Sean, when faced with his cold stare.

Sean moved forward, more than likely to hit him again. If the cretin touched him he would rip the man's arm out of the socket. The look he shot him reflected the thought, and Sean's steps faltered slightly.

"Don't," the boss warned. He turned back to Dmitry. "War is hell, and the cost of freedom is paid for in lives. Regrettable but also unavoidable. Unfortunately, you drew the short straw. Yes, you were expendable. Just a pawn in my game. But you proved to be resourceful. I'll not underestimate you again. Now you will retrieve Sundown for me. Once I confirm it's all there, you and your sister are free to go."

He barely contained his anger at how cavalierly the man spoke of Ivan's murder, as if his friend's life was worth nothing. He glanced in Elena's direction, noticing that she also struggled with her temper.

"What are my guarantees that we'll be let go? We've both seen your faces. I know your name," he said, looking at Sean before returning his cool eyes back to the boss. "And yours will soon come to me, have no doubt about that. How do I know you won't just shoot Elena like you did Ivan?"

"You don't, now do you?" Sean said. "You do as the boss asks, or I'll put a bullet in her brain myself. Are we clear?"

"Although Mr. Henry here lacks diplomacy, I'm afraid he's quite right. There are certain times in a man's life when there are no choices to be made.

That there is only one road you can travel down and that you must obey the rules of which are supplied to you. Believe me, Mr. Ivanov, when I say that in my tenure as a general, there have been many times when I have watched men, women, and children alike murdered for the sake of progress. I have ordered such deaths and I will again if you push me to do so."

Something in his eyes that told Dmitry he wasn't bluffing. Elena offered him a shrug when he glanced in her direction. The trust in her eyes at any decision he would make almost brought him to his knees.

Elena, how the hell do we get into these messes?

"Elena?" he asked, verifying what she wanted him to do. They were heading into dangerous territory and he wanted them to be on the same track.

Elena made herself more comfortable in her chair. When she spoke, it was in a resigned voice. "Just do as they ask, Dmitry. Like the man said, you don't have any other choice."

He could tell she knew Lucas would come for her, that he was probably tearing up all of Virginia, D.C., and Maryland searching for them. He had probably found the GPS by now, and knew Dmitry would find a way to notify him if he got the chance. He had to get a message to Lucas. It would be the only way for them to survive. He knew the men surrounding them were enforcers and that he and Elena wouldn't be leaving the house alive no matter the promises they received. He knew Elena trusted in him and his abilities to get the message across without being seen.

He nodded, making his way to the computer, and sat down in the chair provided. He raised his hands, revealing the handcuffs. The boss shook his head.

"The handcuffs stay on. You're an experienced man, Dmitry, you can make do with what you have. Just for your information, I have with me my assistant, Harrison. He is very good with computers also, though not quite in your caliber, but I doubt many are. If I suspect you are trying to mess with me or Sundown, I will have him review your work. I'm sure you realize the penalty for such an action."

The boss glanced over at Elena, making a not-so-subtle hint. She crossed one leg over the other and let out a scoff full of contempt. The action would have worked better had her wrists not been handcuffed.

"I understand."

"Good. I assume you've made provisions to remove the tag? I think we're all in agreement that we'd like to keep DoD out of this."

Nodding, he turned his attention to the monitor. He began typing, his fingers almost blurring as they moved speedily over the keyboard. He moved into cyberspace and found his last footprint and retraced his steps, uploading the program he'd created the night before. Even with his expertise, it was risky to implement. He'd already seen the DoD's response time, but he had no other choice and hoped since he was only retrieving a small part of the file that they'd lose his thread when he moved on to the next and would have to start the trace over.

He was sure the Pentagon looked like a

Christmas tree right now, with all their bells and whistles going off as he located the first part of Sundown and set it to download. He made short order of finding the first five parts in under ten minutes. The rest would not be so easy, considering he could only access the storage computers hard-drive when the computer was on, otherwise he would have to get creative and send a worm in through a back door to ferret out the file.

The fact that the file had been spread across hundreds of different locations around the world would make it extremely difficult. He had to work on a time restraint, attacking the same time zones at once before moving on. He set about creating the program to do just that, leaving him some time to work on his other quandary.

One of the many problems he had was in not knowing where the hell he was. Not knowing the area. He hadn't been able to visualize a map as they had driven along the Beltway. He was going to need a location to get the cavalry to come save the day. That, and he would need a brilliant idea as to how to let Lucas know where they were without alerting the boss. He would have to be sneaky and overly cautious. They were dead if he was found out.

Bringing up the command box, he flicked through the computer's internal hard-drive and found the IP address for his present location. Using the numbers, he infiltrated the service provider's database and came up with the address. It barely took any time from infiltration to success. He had done so many hacks of this caliber that the entire process could have been completed blindfolded.

The house was registered to the DoD. So far, so good. That was the easy part. The residence was obviously a safe house set up by the government for witnesses and prisoners alike. That was good news as far he was concerned. They would be less inclined to kill them there. They wouldn't want to have to rinse blood out of the carpet; this bought them some time.

I hope.

He glanced at the innocuous round viewer on the top of the monitor. He had an idea. It was just sneaky enough that he might get away with it. He set up the webcam to record and sent a live link to Jim's computer at the CIA. He remembered the address from earlier when he had tried to locate Elena's phone. Moving quickly, he embedded a code that would push through whatever barriers the agency might have.

Chapter 26

Lucas paced back and forth across Jim's office, occasionally looking at the screen of the computer. He trusted Dmitry, knew he would find a way to contact him. The man was smart and resourceful and wouldn't allow a setback to stop him from getting word out.

After the GPS hadn't moved in over an hour, he'd started to worry. *Fuck that*, he'd been downright scared and still was. He'd sent an agent to the last place Dmitry's GPS had placed him—a 7-Eleven. The agent had returned with a pile of clothes, the outfit Dmitry had been wearing.

He'd almost put his fist through the wall and would have had Jim not caught it in time. True fear and panic swelled inside him. He needed to do something—anything. He was a man of action and not designed for sitting on his ass waiting, imagining all the terrible things that could be happening to Elena at that very minute. He continued to pace in order to keep himself occupied, and to keep from tearing up Fitzgibbon's office in futile rage.

If anything happened to Dmitry, he could kiss Elena goodbye, for there was no other reason to keep her alive. The only thing they had to go on was that when Sean had called he had been heading north on the Beltway. Except, there was a hell of a lot of north. The Beltway crossed state lines into D.C. or continued on into Virginia. He felt impotent, unable to do anything to help the woman he loved. He'd waited eighteen months for her and now some bastard was using her as a pawn in a very dangerous game.

Would he ever get a break? He regretted allowing so much time to pass, not wanting to push. They'd let time slip through their fingers. Time he desperately wanted. No woman had ever completed him or tied him in knots like Elena.

The only woman he wanted. The only woman he'd ever loved.

He'd been so close to having it all. He couldn't lose her.

He ran his stiff fingers through his hair. He was extremely frustrated, because of the situation and because he finally felt they both knew where they stood. Last night had been a turning point in their relationship. They had both put their hearts on the line and declared their feelings. He wanted nothing more than to be at home lying next to her in bed, replaying the events of the previous night over and over.

Last night…he almost groaned aloud at the vision dancing in his head. Elena so deliciously naked on his bed, him taking her not once but twice, making her cry out in pleasure, giving to her everything he was and more. Promising her his life and his heart as they made love. Now here, nineteen hours later, he had already lost her to some murdering prick.

His body cooled. Debilitating fear racked his body. It had happened only once before in Russia when Alexei Dimitrovich had kidnapped Elena, deciding to use her as insurance. He hadn't allowed Alexei to hurt her then and he certainly wasn't about to let Sean do that now. They were on his turf, in his country, in his city, and they better be prepared for the consequences. When he found them, he wasn't about to let them go easily, and so help them if they harmed *his* Elena because he could not be held responsible for his actions.

Fitzgibbon's computer beeped, and an incoming video-stream dialog box appeared. Jim frowned, and Lucas stood behind him as a live video feed access request appeared. Jim was about to disregard the message when Lucas stopped him.

"Wait." He looked at the sender's name: Roulette01. He smiled. It had to be Dmitry.

Eighteen months ago, after Dmitry had dropped him and Elena off at Moscow's Leningradsky train station, he'd said to Lucas, *"Remember, if anything happens to her, you are going to have firsthand knowledge of playing Russian roulette, only they'd be more than one bullet, clear?"*

They had been alone when Dmitry had given him the warning; even Elena had no idea what had transpired between the two men. She had been standing outside the vehicle at the time and he'd never spoken a word of it to her. Dmitry wouldn't have shared that with anyone else.

He accepted and the live feed popped up immediately. His assumption proved correct when he viewed the webcam footage. It was Dmitry, his head hiding the rest from view. He looked straight into the camera, giving them a diminutive nod, before he looked to the right and pulled away from the monitor, allowing the webcam to get a shot behind him.

Another man came into view, a man he recognized immediately. The air rushed out his lungs. This was not good, not good at all.

"Is that—?"

The man in the frame was a well-known and well respected man whom Lucas had once liked. He regretted that now. Rage boiled up inside him, the feeling of being betrayed in his mind. This man had indeed betrayed him, and the American people. Betrayed and endangered.

"Leon Gallagher, the National Security Advisor to the President," Jim said, the tone of his voice clipped.

He agreed. "Yes."

Jim lifted his handset and began to dial a number when his computer beeped once more and an instant message appeared. Several words appeared on the screen, making out an address in Rockville, Virginia. He pinched the bridge of his nose as Dmitry followed up with more information telling them that he was in a government safe house and that Elena was okay and to get there quick. He finished the message with an approximate number of men involved. When Lucas brought in the troops, it would be easier to know how many they were dealing with.

He let out a sigh of relief. Elena was safe for now. The knot in his stomach lessened. On the phone, Jim arranged for a team of men to descend upon the peaceful street. He should be there before things turn sour. He didn't trust the other agents not to fire at Elena and Dmitry. They didn't know the two like he did, and he planned to keep them safe. For the rest of their lives.

It would be a tough assignment due to their penchant for trouble, but he was man enough to handle it. Although, it all depended upon Elena, and whether she was prepared and willing to leave everything she had ever known to join him. He prayed she would be up to the task. He moved toward the door, his hand unconsciously going to his weapon holster. He stopped suddenly as a thought entered his head, and he turned around and faced Fitzgibbon.

"I want you to do something for me, Jim," he said. "I want to call in a favor. No, wait…make that two. The man owes Elena and me both."

He explained what he wanted him to do before stepping out the door, mentally preparing himself for the mission ahead. He pushed away all worries, and went into agent mode.

He had a promise to keep.

Chapter 27

Dmitry covered his tracks. Not well, but as best he could under the watchful eye of the National Security Advisor Leon Gallagher. He recognized him now. Not just from television and the news, but from the list of men confirmed to know about Sundown that he'd perused before Lucas had called and interrupted him. He had been so concerned over Elena being taken that he had completely forgotten about going back and looking at it. At least he didn't need to worry about that anymore. His answer was behind him waving a gun like a fanatic.

"You may want to watch him closely, boss," Sean said, breaking the silence. The only sounds heard were the exhaling of breath and Dmitry's typing on the keyboard. The tension was palpable within the room, and Gallagher seemed as tense as a guitar string. "He's a wily one—pulls the wool over your eyes while you watch."

That wasn't hard.

The man was no Einstein, corrupted and living off his street wits. He wondered what Sean got out

180

of his deal with Gallagher. How did he benefit? He thought about it until one word came to him.

Money. He shook his head. He couldn't believe he'd been so stupid. There was only one reason Sean stuck with Gallagher, and it wasn't for the good of the nation. There were only a few things a man like him could do for Gallagher, and it all came back to keeping his hands clean and his nose out of the business. Plausible deniability. Only this time, it went horribly wrong and it would be just like Sean to take advantage of it.

"Tell me something, just out of curiosity. How much are you selling Sundown for and who are the top buyers? North Korea, China, or the Middle East?"

Gallagher turned abruptly. "I am not selling Sundown," he practically screamed. "I am trying to protect this nation. Show those fools in the White House that security is just an illusion, that it's something that can't be bought. You'd think they'd have known that by now."

He could understand the man's passion, how he wanted to protect the country he loved. But that didn't excuse the way he went about showing the nation's vulnerability. There was no reason to go this far. While trying to keep the United States safe, he had put them at risk. He shuddered at how the situation might have played out, had they gotten someone else instead of Dmitry. For a brief second, he was glad they'd chosen him. He was in a position to help the United States, to stop other nations from forcing themselves upon the defenseless country. Then the thought dissipated to be replaced with seething resentment.

"Well, that's too bad, Gallagher," he said. "Because someone in this room is planning on selling Sundown. I wonder if that's before or after they kill you."

Gallagher shook his head, clearly not wanting to believe the truth. Sean turned bright red with anger.

"Impossible," Gallagher snapped. "These men are paid by me. They do as I say."

Dmitry wondered what reality this man lived in. "Well, maybe someone wants a pay rise or a bonus, Gallagher. Ever think of that?"

Gallagher shook his head, glancing at each of his employees. Dmitry could see the doubt fogging his mind, niggling inside his brain, making him question the loyalty of his men.

"Don't listen to him, boss. The man is a liar," Sean said. "He just wants Sundown for himself."

"Then why would I send Sundown all over the world to keep it out of your hands? I believe I'd never heard of it until you came along and shot my friend."

He wished he'd never heard of Sundown; it had caused him nothing but frustration. He had lost a close friend and put his sister at risk. That thought made his stomach churn.

He sent a surreptitious glance to Elena. She was still sitting with her legs crossed, an almost bored expression on her face, but he could see her mind working, plotting an escape if an opportunity presented itself. He knew others underestimated his sister and her many hidden talents, but he'd been knocked on his ass enough times to know she had

182

skills, intelligence, and a bitch of a right hook.

"If you want proof, I can provide it," Dmitry said. "I came across this website when I was looking for you, Gallagher. See for yourself."

He brought up the webpage he had found while at the library. Carefully hidden in the deep, dark web was Sundown's auction. It was going for top dollar, and about to make someone in the room a very rich man. Gallagher moved closer to the screen and quickly read the page. His face contorted with anger before he swung around and aimed his weapon at Sean. The younger man raised his hands in surrender.

"No, boss, it's not me," he said, his manner moving from anger to pleading for his innocence. "I swear I would never do that. It means too much to this country. I would never do anything to harm it."

Gallagher snarled. "If there is nothing I hate more than a liar, it is a traitor. You've been playing me from the very start."

Well, duh.

"What did you fucking expect when you hired a no-good crook? That's what you get. I'm not a caterpillar to turn into a butterfly overnight."

Gallagher squeezed the trigger. The windows shook from the sound of the bullet exiting the chamber. Sean fell to the floor, his sightless eyes staring up at Gallagher. Dmitry glanced over at Elena, whose eyes widened as the National Security Advisor spit on the body, desecrating it. Her nose crinkled, her entire face showing her disgust. She broke off and for an instant her eyes locked with Dmitry's in silent communication. She gave the slightest of nods, agreeing with his plan. All hell was about to break loose and they both knew it.

Gallagher turned once more to him. Beads of sweat dotted his forehead. "What the fuck is taking so long? Why don't you have Sundown back? It's more exposed than ever now that they know it's out there."

Dmitry knew his time was running out. Getting Elena and himself out of there meant he would have to work fast and pray Lucas was not far away. He was on borrowed time. Any passing moment was a blessing.

"Have you any idea the amount of trouble it is to retrieve over a hundred files from computers all around the world? From homes, schools, and offices? It's not as easy as it sounds."

Gallagher looked over at his MIT trained assistant. "Well?"

The young acne-ridden man looked like a deer caught in headlights. Dmitry guessed his age to be early twenties and barely out of college. He'd only just begun to shave, too young to be caught up in this mess. Dmitry felt for him, stuck between love for his country and working with what Dmitry had once thought of as a great man. His gaze shifted from the National Security Advisor to Dmitry before settling once more on Gallagher. "U-uh, y-yes, that's about right, sir," he stammered.

"I don't like it." Gallagher pointed the weapon at Dmitry. "Step away. Harrison, get your ass in there. Tell me how far along he is."

The young man paled, stepping forward nervously as Dmitry moved away. This was not what Harrison had signed on for. He had probably been thinking of a cushy office job with the best computer equipment money could buy. He was certainly mistaken. How unfortunate that he'd thrown his lot in with Gallagher.

Dmitry drew close to Elena, and she watched his face closely, determining the moves he would make so that she could work with him, covering his back if needed. He'd never realized just how well he and Elena worked together until now. It was almost as if they could read each other's minds and completely trusted the other with their lives.

Harrison gingerly sat down in his recently vacated place and began typing. He quickly located the paths that Dmitry had opened and began following them, seeing where they would lead him. Dmitry knew what was coming. Anyone who knew computers could easily track what he'd done since he had not had the chance to delete them. Harrison frowned. He didn't like what he was seeing. Dmitry knew the shit was about to hit the fan big time. He cautiously moved toward Elena, trying to get to her before the tech guy had a chance to tell Gallagher what it was that he had been doing. The man was not about to take the news well and Dmitry wanted Elena out of firing range.

"A-ah sir, there are more lines open here," Harrison said anxiously.

Gallagher glared at the young man. Dmitry could read the distain on his face. Obviously the older man hated tech geeks. Probably because he couldn't understand a word that came out of their mouths. "In English, Harrison," he growled.

Harrison visibly swallowed, his Adams apple bobbing up and down in his throat. When he spoke, his voice was almost as if he was quoting from a textbook or teaching a class. Something Dmitry assumed Gallagher didn't appreciate. Four years of college gone to waste, hadn't the boy taken a social class or something?

"To retrieve Sundown, he would only need to be working with a few open lines and use more commands on those that are open. To have as many up as Mr. Ivanov does will only slow the download speed and make it take that much longer."

Harrison typed fast into the command box, clearly well versed on the keyboard and knowledge of the computer. He followed the steps Dmitry had made. His frown deepened as he worked, his concentration completely on the task before him. Dmitry imagined him bringing up the main page he'd been working on and the file transfer box telling him it was at sixty-five percent. He continued his quest to find what else he'd had been working on. Dmitry knew the steps the kid would make and knew the moment Harrison located the webcam file and watched as the kid nervously nibbled on his bottom lip.

Harrison opened the command file and found the open channel. From the angle, Dmitry could just make out the Harrison's reflection as the webcam was brought up on screen. He silently signaled to Elena who gave an almost indiscernible nod. She was ready.

"Ah sir you should see this. I think we have a problem," Harrison said, his voice nervous.

Gallagher glared at the boy. He moved across the small space dividing them and breathed down Harrison's neck, the action causing Harrison to squirm like a little boy needing to go to the bathroom.

"I-I found this. It's been broadcasting," Harrison said as he revealed the webcam to Gallagher.

The Security Advisor sucked in air as he drew a startled breath as he too came face to face with his reflection. He watched as his face on screen moved at the same time he did. He stared almost dumbfounded at the mirror image before it clicked inside his mind. The man's jaw clenched and he turned toward him, his weapon pointing straight at Dmitry's heart.

Elena surged to her feet. She glanced his way, stark fear etched on her face. She was probably thinking she was about to lose him just as she'd done with Nikolai and he prayed she didn't act foolishly. It wasn't over yet.

"What have you done? Do you realize what this means? Everything I have done is finished. The country is ruined, all because of you," Gallagher yelled at him from a mere few feet away, certainly not far enough to warrant screaming. The vein in his temple pulsated and the cords in his neck were tight. The man was as mad as a rattlesnake and just as deadly. "Where does that feed go? Where did you send it?" he ground out, spittle flying from his mouth.

Dmitry sensed the panic rising within him. There was no escaping the cold hard fact. The man was screwed. It didn't matter where that feed went or to whom. He was found out and he would never be able to go back to his job or to the life he once had. He was finished and would most likely be tried for treason.

"Langley. It's been on for the past half hour or so. You're well recognizable, sir, so I doubt they had trouble identifying you. Every law enforcement officer in the state is on the way here. You should give up now and quit while you're ahead."

Gallagher's face wrinkled in rage. "It's because of countries like yours, Russian, that has made all this necessary, but you made one big fucking mistake and that was fucking with me."

He turned his weapon on Elena just as the perimeter alarms went off. Dmitry lunged at his sister, knocking her off her feet as a bullet whizzed past them, missing them by centimeters.

Chapter 28

Dmitry felt the heat as another bullet flew by before imbedding in the wall behind him. He cursed savagely. With his hands handcuffed, he navigated Elena to cover, dodging the other bullets Gallagher let off, determined to hit them in his frustration.

On their hands and knees, he and Elena moved quickly toward the other side of the room removing themselves from harm's way, crawling behind a sofa while trying to keep out of the path of rapidly fired bullets. Puffs of foam from inside the sofa rained down on them as the bullets easily soared through the back support. He and Elena kissed the floor, going down onto their stomachs sliding along the well varnished hardwood floor like they were army cadets doing basic training making their way through the mud.

His face reflected back at him from the polished hardwood floor beneath him. The expression was concern mixed with anger. He'd had enough and if it weren't for Elena he would have been trying to diffuse the situation but he didn't want to leave her for a second. Bad things tended to happen when she was unsupervised. Elena would have hit him had she heard his thought and then argued until she was blue in the face that it wasn't her fault. The woman had the worse luck in the world. He felt the wood shavings settle on the back of his neck as two more bullets were dispelled into the couch.

Forcing his mind back to their current predicament, he glanced over his shoulder to ensure Elena was still following and unharmed. She was and wore an aggrieved look on her face. He had to stall and buy the boys in blue some time. It shouldn't be long now. They had already breached the security perimeter and the alarm was blaring in warning providing an almost deafening colophony with the bullets.

The sound of a magazine hitting the floor had him picking up speed, crawling now in hopes of getting to safety before the man had a chance to reload. The floor was hard on his knees, rubbing at his skin and irritating it. He blocked out the pain and focused on getting himself and Elena out of the way before all hell broke loose.

***

Elena moved quickly behind Dmitry, keeping her head low and out of firing range. She could feel the splinters imbedding into her soft palms. She gritted her teeth and fought the urge to stop and pull them out. She followed her brother, trusting him to get them out of danger. The rain of fire they were under had momentarily ceased while Gallagher reloaded his weapon. Her ears rung from the constant popping sound of the gun discharging and the alarm blaring. Her wrists were sore from the handcuffs and she was still feeling the lingering effects of the taser. She couldn't see anything ahead of her besides Dmitry crawling and didn't dare look back.

Afraid to lose her rhythm she kept her eyes glued in front of her. So focused on her task, she had no warning he was behind her. The hairs on the back of her neck rose a moment too late. He grabbed her as she crawled, yanking her off her feet. She let out a startled scream and cursed herself for being caught off guard again. She'd been taught better than that. Her feet dangled futilely as the man with the dragon tattoo wrapped his bulky arms around her chest, hugging her from behind, effectively pinning her arms to her sides. She winced and knew she would have bruises tomorrow from where Dragon Man held her that would surely blend in nicely with her rapidly growing collection.

Why does this keep happening to me?

She bucked wildly using her entire strength and will to live against the behemoth of a man. Dragon Man squeezed her hard, winding her. She fought for breath, having none. She imagined her face turning purple as he continued to hold onto her tightly. She struggled as she felt the darkness threatening to swamp her once more. As she bucked against the steel hard chest of her attacker she heard a large clunk as Dragon Man's gun fell loudly to the floor when it slipped from his waistband at the small of his back. It was followed by a scraping sound as the man's foot found the gun and unintentionally sent it flying across the room as she fought back, distracting him until he was entirely focused on her. She fought even harder and wilder, refusing to be rendered unconscious for the second time that day. She kicked back, putting as much force as she could into the attack, her sneakers connecting with his knees and she felt his legs buckle beneath her.

Her head jerked back, hitting Dragon Man's chin hard with the top of her head. His teeth slammed together, his jaw shattering even as her vision swam before her eyes. He cried out in pain as he dropped her. She moved quickly remembering the skills Nikolai had burned into her head, stamping down hard on his instep before landing an elbow to his stomach and then to the nose. Bones cracked under the strain and blood spurted out. She finished him off with a knee to the groin before side stepping out of the man's reach. She watched as he groped himself, as if cupping his family jewels would stop the hurting if he applied pressure to them. Elena smiled heartlessly. The routine always worked like a charm. Too bad if the man ever wanted kids, her inner voice quipped. She'd done the world a favor. If there was anyone who should not reproduce it was that guy.

"Why does no one remember that *I'm* an agent also?" she asked, astonished, as she regulated her breathing, her lungs no longer screaming for oxygen. It always seemed to her that she was being kidnapped or treated like some blonde haired bimbo in a movie, always expected to scream for help or breaking her ankle as she tried to escape. She was more than capable of looking out for herself as Dragon Man had just discovered. Her husband had been an SVR agent for Christ's sake. He taught her every self-defense move he knew. She could certainly handle herself.

She glanced down at Dragon Man who was still lying on the floor in a fetal position, blood marring the pristine wax job. He had one hand on his genitals and the other on his nose. Tears fell from his eyes mixing in with the blood as he swore. Satisfaction momentarily filled her, quickly disappearing when he glared up at her with a promise of retribution in his eyes. He climbed to his feet in one swift motion, his teeth grinding together in pain. He made one threatening step forward before taking two steps back, his eyes wide with shock as a loud boom shook the room. A neat red hole appeared on his chest right above his heart before he collapsed in a heap on the floor.

She swung around, her mouth open in an *O* as she took in her little brother. His eyes were cold and narrow, firmly attached to the dead man on the floor nearby. The gun in his hand trained toward the motionless body, waiting for any slight movement telling him the man was still alive. She shivered slightly as she saw the look in his eyes. Dmitry had never looked so primitive, so cold and deadly. He looked every bit the scary Russian he'd often been charged of being. She'd told Lucas Dmitry could be cold and indifferent but this was a new facet. She had a sudden insight into the man who was her brother, the man who would do anything to protect those he loved.

193

She was still processing what her brother had just done for her when his heavy weight suddenly slammed into her, knocking her off her feet before making contact with the hard surface of the floor. Dmitry rolled and covered her protectively with his body just as the front door of the safe house was barreled open. FBI agents forced their way inside, their AK-47s at the ready as they entered, shooting those who resisted, swarming through every entrance. Glass shattered as windows were broken and doors hung precariously from one hinge as they were rammed.

Gallagher's eyes bulged as he took in the federal SWAT team. His face turned desperate as he spun around at the men surrounding him. Before anyone registered what he was about to do, their attention solely on rounding up the men with guns and detaining them, the National Security Adviser raised his arm and squeezed the trigger before he could be stopped. For the last time that day the sound of a bullet exiting the chamber filled the room followed by the scent of a recently discharged weapon. Every eye in the room turned its focus on Gallagher as his lifeless body hit the soiled carpet beneath him.

Elena jerked unconsciously from what she'd just witnessed and her stomach rolled. She closed her eyes in an effort to block out the sight of fresh blood and brain matter. It was something she never wanted to see again. When this was all over she was going on a vacation—a proper one hopefully with a beach and free-flowing alcohol.

She opened her eyes as an FBI agent stepped

gingerly over to the body, kicking the gun away, moving it out of reach before he squatted down beside Gallagher and checked futilely for a pulse. He shook his head, addressing the room at large who were all watching him. The rest of the FBI SWAT team turned back to their duties, knowing there was nothing they could do for the man.

Chapter 29

Lucas entered the residence last. Since this was not his bust he had been relegated to the back. He'd not liked it one bit and had made his displeasure known but even that had not changed the FBI Agent in Charge's mind. His sharp, alert eyes moved across the room taking everything in as he searched for Elena. His gaze found her as a young agent helped her to her feet. He drank her in, from her pale hair in disarray right down to her sneakered feet. Considering what she had been through and witnessed she was looking quite well. Although, Lucas had to admit, Elena could put up with a hell of a lot and still be up for more. The woman had marvelous perseverance as he had witnessed on more than one occasion in their time together.

He strode across the room to get to her, the desire to hold onto her tight and never let go overwhelming him. If he thought she would let him, he would lock her away in his house where no one could hurt her. He realized the stupidity of that thought immediately. She had been taken from his house. He would amend that as soon as he got home and make it safe once more. A place she would want to stay—permanently if he had his way.

She looked over at him and smiled brilliantly before catapulting herself into his arms, her handcuffed wrists stealing around his neck, the cool of the stainless steel sliding against his skin. She kissed him with the same passion she had the night before, leaving nothing of her feelings for him questioned. He loved how uninhibited she was. He kissed her back with the same amount of passion, matching her, wrapping his arms around her waist, holding her close to him. Her feet hung limply, several inches off the floor as he lifted her into his embrace unable to remain even a breath away from her. He'd almost lost her again. He wasn't chancing a third. He didn't know what he'd do without her. She was a part of him and his heart belonged entirely to her. He tightened his arms around her, his entire concentration on the way her tongue mated with his with a promise of things to come.

"Will you two get a room?" Dmitry interrupted as he came up behind Elena, unclipping the handcuffs from his wrists and sliding them an amused glance.

Elena detangled herself from him and stumbled back. He caught hold of her arm to steady her and simply because he couldn't not touch her. His fingertips tingled as they connected with her soft flesh. She refused to look at him as she attempted to straighten her clothes and finger comb her hair, obviously trying to regain some of her dignity. He could've told her she was long past that but decided against it. He was hardly a stupid man. He caught sight of the handcuffs binding her wrists and shook his head.

"Handcuffs again, Elena?" He grinned at her and lowered his voice an octave. "You should have told me you had an affinity for them. I would've used them last night."

He waggled his eyebrows playfully.

***

Elena fought the blush, not at all amused. She hit him hard on the shoulder, smiling sweetly when he winced, not particularly caring for handcuffs. The last pair she'd worn had cut her skin as she'd contorted her body to be free of them so she could help Lucas defuse the situation they'd found themselves in on board Alexei's boat. The reminder brought back memories of a colder time. Yet, thankfully, there had been a light to the darkness— meeting Lucas. Now she couldn't even imagine what her life would've been like otherwise.

He gently took hold of her wrist and unlocked each handcuff, setting her free. He kissed each wrist, his mouth lingering on the sensitive flesh on the inside. She shivered as he made something so simple erotic. Her blood heated and her heartbeat sped up. She tensed, her body melting and wanted nothing more than to be alone with Lucas. He must have sensed where her thoughts had gone because after a moment of hesitation he stepped back, breaking the sensual tidal wave in which she had gotten caught in.

Looking up at his face she noted with pleasure that his breathing was irregular and that his eyes had darkened with desire. She glanced away from the promises she saw clear as day on his face and over his broad shoulder, stilling as her gaze settled on the entourage coming straight toward them. A man impeccably dressed in an expensive Ralph Lauren suit was flanked by six men all packing heat and unreadable expressions.

She and Lucas immediately moved to stand side by side providing a buffer between the men and Dmitry. She loved that they thought the same way and that no matter who they faced they did it together and that he protected Dmitry as if he were his own brother. She hadn't thought she could love Lucas any more than she already did, but her heart swelled with such love that she felt as if she could float away.

She recognized one of the men as the agent of the Secret Service whom she had given an antique axe after it appeared all the fire exits of the Winter Palace in St Petersburg had been rigged to close, designed to keep them trapped inside. He appeared to remember her as well as he gave her a smile and a wink. Lucas stiffened beside her. She looked away from the Secret Service Agent to the man they were protecting. It was hard not to recognize the President of the United States. He was a handsome man in his late forties who carried himself well. Of all the broadcasts she had heard, he spoke rather eloquently with a slight southern brogue left over from his formative years in Louisiana.

The president stopped before them. He looked

from her to Lucas. "Agent Gates, Agent Ivanova, a pleasure. I hear the country owes you quite the debt of gratitude. I more than anyone. It appears you have once more averted disaster. It seems to be becoming a habit of yours. I'm exceedingly thankful for your efforts in stopping Sundown from being leaked or sold. I'm sure you understand the severity of the situation had you not intercepted."

Lucas nodded, accepting the gratitude, although she knew no thanks was needed. To men like him he saw it as only doing his job to keep the homeland safe but this was the second time in the not so distant past he had gone beyond the call of duty and she was exceedingly proud of him.

While the president barely gave more than a brief glance about the room, she knew he was taking everything in. His gaze finally settled over her left shoulder where Dmitry stood.

"Dmitry Ivanov, I suppose?" he asked. "I've heard a lot about you."

Dmitry stepped forward, shouldering his way between her and Lucas. She wanted to stop him. To hide him away. He was her little brother and it was her job to protect and care for him. She'd failed. She watched with pride as he stood to his full height, unafraid and ready to accept his punishment. She remembered him doing the same as a small boy. He took his responsibilities serious and always faced the repercussions of any act with remarkable aplomb. He held out his hand, and the president shook it.

"Mr. President," Dmitry said reverently.

The president nodded, his sharp eyes scrutinizing

Dmitry. Elena's heart beat painfully in her chest and she trembled with fear. Dmitry didn't deserve to be punished for an act he would not have committed under normal circumstances. He was a decent man who may have dabbled in grey areas but never for profit or terror. Whatever happened, she knew she would never stop fighting until he was released.

Lucas gently touched her elbow before stepping forward, making his movement as non-threatening as possible as to not alarm the Secret Service but also to draw the President's attention to him and away from Dmitry.

"Mr. President, I'd like to speak on behalf of Dmitry. He's a good, honest man who was a victim of circumstance. He should not be blamed for the theft but instead commended for its safe keeping. If it weren't for him, Sundown would more than likely be in the hands of our enemies right now."

Heart thumping in her chest, she blinked back the tears threatening to embarrass her.

No matter what happened today she'd always be grateful to Lucas for backing Dmitry; his reputation and integrity was well respected throughout the Intelligence community.

She hugged herself tightly, needing reassurance that all would be well, knowing it was far from it and that this man held her brother's future in his hands. Her stomach spasmed painfully as she waited for the president to speak.

"I agree," the president said. "The United States is indeed indebted to Mr. Ivanov and extremely grateful for his involvement. I had a long talk with SAC Fitzgibbon and he too spoke on your behalf. It seems there are many who sing your praises. I've spoken to the US Attorney and your case has been dropped and your record expunged. Just don't go hacking any more government sites."

Elena exhaled; she hadn't realized she'd been holding her breath. "Thank you, Mr. President. You have no idea what this means to me—to us."

He smiled back at her. "No, I think I do, Agent Ivanova. I have a younger brother myself. Well, I must be off. I am a busy man, you know. Have a country to run and all. Again, thank you—all of you."

After watching him leave, she turned to the two men in her life. It all seemed so surreal. The fear they'd lived in for the past few days gone. Dmitry looked about the room, his body relaxed, and his demeanor lighter despite all that had transpired. She would never forget what he'd done for her or the look on his face shortly after he'd killed a man to protect her.

Her gaze followed his. The FBI agents Lucas had brought with him were currently escorting the National Security Advisor's lackeys out the door in handcuffs. The young tech, Harrison, was wide eyed as he took in the fact that the man he had worked for had tried to steal a security protocol and kill innocent people.

"Good might not always triumph but technology is here to help," Dmitry said.

She shook her head. If there was any religion her brother believed in it was technology. His philosophy was that you could do just about anything with a computer and there were always men out there like him who were there to clean up after the ones who used that fact to their advantage.

Lucas's cell vibrated and he retrieved it from his belt before answering it with his usual style—which meant no pleasantries at all. He caught her gaze, his eyebrow raised. "Elena, I have Director Mishkin on the phone. He would like to talk to you."

Elena grimaced and seriously considered ignoring him. This wasn't a conversation she wanted to have. She knew exactly what the SVR Director wanted to say but wasn't interested in hearing it. She nibbled on her lower lip, deciding whether or not to take the call then decided to get it over with. It would do no good to delay the inevitable. She took the phone from Lucas and put it to her ear.

"Director Mishkin," she said crisply into the phone before moving the phone away from her ear as a tirade of loud Russian came through. She glanced over at Dmitry and made a face. Her brother looked pained as he shamelessly listened to every word. Lucas, too, watched her face closely. Probably trying to read her expression to decipher what was being said. He'd just have to be patient. She let out a deep breath and waited for the Director to finish. A moment later she delicately hung up the phone feeling ragged and despondent.

"Elena, I'm so sorry." Dmitry spoke first. His voice soothing, his face riddled with guilt. "You should not have jeopardized your career for me."

She smiled at him. "It's not your fault, Dmitry. He would have done it sooner or later. I don't play by his rules and cause ripples in his perfect world."

She and Mishkin had never seen eye to eye after he'd approved the verdict on her husband's murder as a simple case of burglary gone bad. She'd never agreed and had voiced that opinion and ruffled his feathers until he'd benched her from active duty, only reinstating her when Lucas arrived six months later as no one in the office had wanted to work with an American.

For a time, after the St Petersburg incident they had existed in harmony but her time with Lucas had irrevocably changed her—unfavorably so in Mishkin's opinion. She no longer followed the rules to the letter and that grated on him who was the very embodiment of procedures. He liked a tidy world and she had disrupted it.

Lucas looked from one to the other. "What's going on?"

Elena shrugged. "Director Mishkin just wanted to say in no uncertain terms…" Her voice broke.

Her brother half hugged her, his arm draping across her shoulder and giving her a squeeze. "He fired her."

"What?" Lucas was outraged. "Give me that phone. I'll talk to Mishkin and smooth things over. Under the circumstances—"

She kissed him, effectually shutting him up. "I don't care." She shook her head. "No, that's a lie. I do care. But it's not important. It's just a job and I would do the same thing all over again knowing the end result."

She smiled at Dmitry again before turning to Lucas. "So, is there still room at the Gates hotel?" she joked to cover the underlining vulnerability she felt. She was feeling lost without purpose, unsure of her role in life—his life. She knew he wanted her but did that extend to every moment for the foreseeable future? She might outstay her welcome when he discovers some of her less delightful quirks and habits.

He pulled her into his solid chest, holding her close. She inhaled his unique scent, feeling as if she were home. He kissed her hard, taking his time. Reminding her of everything they had shared. The whole world blurred around until there was only Lucas. When she finally broke away, they were both breathing heavily.

Fighting for breath, she heard him say, "Always for you, *sladkaya*, always for you."

Epilogue

Two Days Later…
CIA Headquarters
Langley, Virginia, USA

Elena stood beside Lucas in SAC Fitzgibbon's office. The man had just finished verifying the charges against her brother had been completely dropped, as promised. She felt an invisible weight lift from her chest, one she hadn't even been aware of. The evening news had reported the untimely death of the National Security Advisor in a single motor vehicle accident and the country mourned for him. There was no mention of the DoD being hacked or the theft of project Sundown.

She wasn't surprised. The last thing the government wanted was for the public to know how vulnerable they'd been just days ago nor that a well-respected man had initiated the incident. Sometimes it was best to keep some secrets from the light of day and it had all worked out in the end and that was all that mattered.

She wore jeans and a blouse, her pale hair hanging loosely around her shoulders. It was a rather impromptu meeting. Had she known she would be standing at Langley she would've dressed for the occasion. Lucas stood beside her similarly dressed and at ease. He'd taken a few days off to spend time with her. This was the first time they had gotten out of bed for anything besides food. She felt delightfully exhausted and knew she must be glowing from sheer happiness—and good sex.

Dmitry had moved out into a hotel while he toured D.C. She knew he wanted to give her and Lucas as much alone time together as possible and she loved her brother for it. Secretary Mann had been overjoyed to have Sundown back. Since no one actually got a look at the contents, he'd determined the protocol was still valid, and he ensured it was about as secure as it could get. He had even asked Dmitry for suggestions and had taken on one of his own security programs to keep it safe.

"Well, thank you very much, Jim, for all your help," Elena said.

He smiled, the skin around his eyes crinkling. She was more grateful to him than she could express. If it weren't for him and Lucas, she didn't want to think what might've happened. She owed a lot to them both.

"And you, Elena. It was a pleasure, I assure you," Jim stated. "I've worked with your countrymen before. You're a hard lot. Give it as good as you get, though. But you're also loyal and I'm proud to be counted among your friends. I must say I've never seen Secretary Mann get put down so eloquently in my entire time here at the agency. You have quite the talent, which leads me to something I'd like to ask you."

Elena raised her eyebrow and waited.

Lucas snorted. "Now that you're sufficiently buttered up."

"Can it, Gates." Jim shot him a glare. "On behalf of the CIA, I would formally like to invite you into our little club. We could use a good liaison and I heard you were between jobs."

Her heart raced. An opportunity to stay here with Lucas. She would be crazy not to grab hold of it with both hands. The last few days, she'd been feeling adrift, unsure of her future. While Lucas went out of his way to show her that she belonged here with him, she hated being idle and couldn't stand the thought of being a kept woman. She wanted to contribute to her life with Lucas, to the country, and to the world.

Lucas scoffed and Jim shot him another look to be quiet. Like always, he didn't heed the warning. "She'd make a fine commodity to the agency, what with all her contacts around the world."

"We all have our strengths," Jim agreed. "Elena is a fine agent and I heard she would be staying in Washington for some time." He looked Lucas in the eye, waiting to see if he would deny it. He didn't. "Dmitry has already accepted my offer of employment. It appears you aren't the only one who plans to stay."

Her eyes widened in shock. If there was one thing her brother always said, it was that no government would ever rule him. Incredulously, she asked, assuming she heard wrong, "Dmitry is going to be working for the CIA?"

Jim shrugged. "We thought it best to have him on our side, working with us rather than against. He got a good package too and is already filling out the employment forms and visa application."

She let out a deep breath. "And just how did you manage that?"

Jim shrugged like it was no big deal, just an ordinary everyday occurrence. "Oh, you know, I promised him if he signed on I would drop the hacker charges and involuntary endangerment...the president left those off the original immunity document."

She scowled. "I hope he didn't fall for that and give his countrymen all a bad name."

"Hell no," Jim grinned. "He told me to go get stuffed."

She nodded. "That's more like it. Well, then, boss...I accept."

Lucas grinned. Jim shook his head at his obvious pleasure. She turned toward Lucas and kissed him soundly. "I know," she told him. "Me too."

He looked deep into her eyes and saw the love for her reflected in his gorgeous blue ones. He made her feel alive and cherished. That she was the only woman in the world for him. After Nikolai, she had thought she would never feel this way again and knew he would approve of Lucas. He would not want her to be sad and lonely and live a life full of regrets. She would never forget Nikolai. He was her first love and had been taken entirely too soon but he was a part of her past now and her future was right in front of her and looking more promising by the minute.

Everything seemed to be coming together. She and Lucas were finally on the path they were meant to be on and now Dmitry was remaining close. She had everything she could possibly want.

"One thing, though," Lucas said, breaking into her thoughts. "It will be a cold day in hell before you'll be decorating *our* home."

Her eyes narrowed as she immediately took offense. She broke away from their embrace, her hands automatically going to her hips. How dare he insult her decorating skills. Sure, she wasn't Martha Stewart, but who the hell was? Although she admitted to herself her home-making skills were less than desirable but *he* sure as hell shouldn't be saying so.

"Surely I couldn't do worse than you," she threw back. "What do they call your decorating style, anyway? 'Early American college boy'?"

"Beautiful and quick witted. I can't go wrong," Lucas said.

Jim cleared his throat. "One more thing before you leave. My wife, Maggie, would like to invite you both to dinner. She seems fascinated with you, Elena, and can't wait to meet the woman who captured Lucas's heart."

She grinned and stared into Lucas's eyes. "I did, didn't I?"

"You sure did."

***

Two Years Later…
Annandale, Virginia, USA

The message light blinked as though going into cardiac arrest. Elena bounded over to the answering machine, thinking maybe her husband had called to let her know when he'd be home. They had been married for almost two years and had a beautiful daughter. Life couldn't be better. To think, she'd once been so worried that he'd lost interest in her. Lucas made sure she knew how much he loved her every day.

Smiling, she pressed the play button, her body stiffening when a woman's voice came on the line, slightly breathless.

"Hi Elena. It's Carey…Carey Madigan. I really need to talk to you. I know it's been a while, but I need your help. I have nowhere else to turn, please call me as soon as you get this…*please*." She emphasized and ended the call with her cell number.

Elena's heart constricted. Carey sounded so anxious and tense, like she was barely holding on. What could've happened to cause her to reach out so desperately? Carey had always been so level-headed, but she didn't sound like herself on the voice mail message. Whatever was troubling her, Elena vowed to help her through it. For Carey to be calling, it had to be bad. She would not fail her again.

"Oh my," she murmured.

Acknowledgments

I'd like to thank Limitless Publishing and their wonderful staff who make the road to publishing fun and seamless. I appreciate all their assistance and support. To the many blogs who have helped spread the word about my books, thank you so much.

I'd also like to thank you, the reader. I hope you enjoyed *American Law* as much as I enjoyed writing it.

About the Author

Camille Taylor is an Australian author who resides in the Nation's Capital with her small dog. She was the typical 90's kid and was raised on Goosebumps, Roald Dahl and Paul Jennings. In her teens she began reading the Queen of Crime, Agatha Christie and in later years found Christine Feehan, Janet Evanovich and Julie Garwood.

She started writing at sixteen and enjoys spending time with her family, doting on her nieces and nephews, writing the many stories floating about her head and working on her genealogy where she can trace her heritage to England, Scotland, Ireland and Russia.

Her other interests include, anything creative—such as scrapbooking and drawing and has travelled across Western Europe, New Zealand and the UAE, after spending a year living in London. She's also dabbled in tae kwon do.

Facebook:
https://www.facebook.com/CamilleTaylorAuthor

Twitter:
https://twitter.com/CamilleTaylorAu

Website:
https://camilletaylorbooks.wordpress.com/

Goodreads:
https://www.goodreads.com/author/show/7791241.
Camille_Taylor